DIAL BOOKS FOR YOUNG READERS
A division of Penguin Young Readers Group
Published by The Penguin Group
Penguin Group (USA) Inc., 375 Hudson Street,
New York, NY 10014, U.S.A.
(Canada), 90 Eglinton Avenue East, Suite 700, Toronto, Ontario,
la M4P 2Y3 (a division of Pearson Penguin Canada Inc.)
uin Books Ltd, 80 Strand, London WC2R 0RL, England
guin Ireland, 25 St. Stephen's Green, Dublin 2, Ireland
(a division of Penguin Books Ltd)
p (Australia), 250 Camberwell Road, Camberwell, Victoria 3124,
stralia (a division of Pearson Australia Group Pty Ltd)
enguin Books India Pvt Ltd, 11 Community Centre,
Panchsheel Park, New Delhi - 110 017, India
Group (NZ), 67 Apollo Drive, Rosedale, Auckland 0632,
ew Zealand (a division of Pearson New Zealand Ltd)
ooks (South Africa) (Pty) Ltd, 24 Sturdee Avenue, Rosebank,
Johannesburg 2196, South Africa
Penguin Books Ltd, Registered Offices: 80 Strand,
London WC2R 0RL, England

Book design by Jasmin Rubero
Text set in Breughel T
Printed in the U.S.A.

1 3 5 7 9 10 8 6 4 2

Library of Congress Cataloging-in-Publication Data
Bransford, Nathan
Jacob Wonderbar and the cosmic space kapow /
by Nathan Bransford ; illustrated by C. S. Jennings
p.   cm.
en sixth-grade classroom terror Jacob Wonderbar and his friends
xter find a spaceship crashed in the woods near their suburban
heir discovery leads them to a series of adventures including space
travel, substitute teachers, kidnapping, and more.

ISBN 978-0-8037-3537-8 (hardcover)
e and adventurers—Fiction. 2. Interplanetary voyages—Fiction.
e teachers—Fiction. 4. Behavior—Fiction. 5. Fathers—Fiction.]
I. Jennings, C. S., ill. II. Title
PZ7.B73755Jac 2011
[Fic]—dc22
2010038152

JAC
WON

Penguin Grou
Can
Pen
Pe

Penguin Gr
A

Peng

Penguin

Summary:
Sarah and
neighborhoo

[1. Adve
3. Subs

DIAL BOOKS F
an imprint o

CHAPTER 1

Each type of substitute teacher had its own special weakness, and Jacob Wonderbar knew every possible trick to distract them. Male substitutes with long hair and women in tie-dyed skirts often had a guitar stashed nearby and were just waiting for an excuse to ditch the lesson plan and play a song. The mousy ones who spoke softly and tentatively when they introduced themselves would patiently answer every absurd question Jacob asked them and would be confronting a classroom gone wild within minutes.

Older subs were more challenging. Having endured a lifetime of rowdy classrooms, they better understood that children were their mortal enemies. They came to class early and peered out warily through thick glasses, ready for battle. They armed themselves with ancient metal thermoses and cranky dispositions.

Jacob sized up the new sub and wondered if he had finally met his match. She was impossibly tall and thin, with a wart on both cheeks and a glint of evil in her eye. She wore a long faded dress with a hideous floral print. Her shoes were clunky and beige. Everything about her seemed crooked: Her fingers were spindly, her posture was hunched, her nose was bent. She had a crooked set of yellow teeth and foul breath that smelled like burned coffee and rotten eggs.

He watched carefully as she scrawled "Mrs. Pinkerton" on the chalkboard and underlined it six times with increasing ferocity. Her handwriting dripped with malice.

She was the scariest substitute teacher he had ever seen.

With a lurching twitch, Mrs. Pinkerton cleared her voice, a mixture of gravel and syrup, and warbled, "Good morning, class."

Jacob's classmates were too scared to reply. He knew they were counting on him to gain the upper hand. He was Jacob Wonderbar, substitute teacher slayer extraordinaire. He had forced more subs to flee the classroom than he could count. His mission was simple: Distract the substitute from the lesson plan without getting sent to the principal's office. Bonus points for making them reconsider their choice of profession and/or purpose in life.

Mrs. Pinkerton smiled, sending a chill down Jacob's spine, and warbled again, louder this time, "I said good morning, class."

A few of Jacob's classmates answered with a quiet, nervous, "Good morning, Mrs. Pinkerton."

Jacob looked over at Dexter, his trusty friend with messy brown hair and a perpetual look of fear in his eyes. Jacob whispered, "This is not good."

Suddenly a ruler appeared in Mrs. Pinkerton's hands and she furiously rapped a table. "I. Heard. That." Silence filled the classroom. Dexter buried his head in his arms.

Mrs. Pinkerton slinked over to Jacob's desk. She appeared to grow taller with every step. She loomed over Jacob, and he smelled her fearsome breath. "Are you Jacob Wonderbar?"

Jacob smiled at her rookie mistake. Never let a sixth grader identify himself. He shook his head. "No, sorry, you have the wrong . . ."

Mrs. Pinkerton cackled without smiling. The back of Jacob's neck prickled. "Of course you are. I've been *warned* about you."

She turned to walk back to the front of the class but

suddenly whirled around, leaned forward, and jabbed a crooked finger in front of Jacob's face. "I'm watching you," she whispered.

Jacob felt a sudden pain on his earlobe, which could only have meant one thing. Sarah had flicked it.

Sarah sat behind Jacob. She was a very pretty girl with piercing blue eyes and golden hair, and the one thing in the entire world that drove her the craziest was when people called her by both her first and last name, "Sarah Daisy." She said it made her sound like the girliest girl on the planet. Needless to say, she did not appreciate it when Jacob passed her a note that said, simply, "Sarah DAISY."

Sarah flicked his ear again, even harder than the last time.

"I HEARD THAT!" Mrs. Pinkerton shouted. As she stomped over to Jacob's desk again, he smiled at his good luck. Sarah never got into trouble, and this time she was caught red-handed. Getting in trouble would make her mad, and Jacob found her quite hilarious when she was mad. Which of course only made her angrier.

"Jacob Wonderbar, you have two strikes."

"Me? She was the one—"

"Zip it!"

"But—"

"Zip!"

"I—"

"ZIP!"

Jacob slumped back in his seat. Dexter raised his head out of his arms and shook it slowly, warning Jacob not to push it this time. He knew what Jacob was thinking before Jacob knew what Jacob was thinking. Then Dexter buried his head in his arms again.

Jacob shook off Dexter's warning. He waited until Mrs. Pinkerton was facing the chalkboard and coughed *"Pinkerton"* into his arm, hoping to inspire the class into a sudden fake coughing fit.

"Demerit," Mrs. Pinkerton immediately coughed back before any of Jacob's classmates could so much as inhale. She walked over to Miss Banks's demerit chart and moved Jacob's card five slots to the right, an unexplored region of demeritdom that he had previously assumed was only reserved for criminals.

Jacob's ears burned as he weighed his options. He thought about his mom, at work in some hotshot meeting probably. He knew that if he was sent to the principal's office it would mean she would be called out of work, then she'd arrive at the principal's office with a red tint in her cheeks, and when they got in the car his mom would look straight ahead and say, "I don't want to say anything I'll regret later," and then they'd ride home in complete silence. He had already promised to never land himself in the principal's office ever again.

But Mrs. Pinkerton had to be stopped.

"Dexter Goldstein?" Mrs. Pinkerton called out.

One eye appeared out from Dexter's tangled arms. "Present?"

Mrs. Pinkerton rapped her knuckles on her desk. "I am *not* calling roll. It is science time. I must insist that you stand in front of the class and recite the first fifty elements of the periodic table."

Jacob's class had only studied the first ten elements. Dexter shook his head, since there must have been a mix-up. "But we—"

"There is no mistake!" Mrs. Pinkerton yelled. "And I'd hate to think what would happen if you were to get one wrong."

After hesitating for a moment, Dexter slumped out of his chair and stood in front of the class. He gazed out the window and Jacob assumed that he was considering the possibility of an escape. Dexter looked at Jacob with an expression that said: "These twelve years have been nice and everything, but I am definitely going to die at the front of this classroom."

"Well?" Mrs. Pinkerton asked.

Dexter stared at his feet. "Um . . . Hydrogen?"

"WRONG!" Mrs. Pinkerton thundered. "I do not

see *umhydrogen* anywhere on the periodic table. I suggest you try again without stuttering."

Jacob heard Sarah take a deep breath. The class was completely silent. Dexter's face was pale.

"Hydrogen," Dexter whispered.

"Correct," Mrs. Pinkerton said. "Next?"

"Um . . ."

The class gasped.

Dexter held up his hands. "I mean, not um. Definitely not um. Starting over. Pretend I didn't say that word that I definitely . . . did not say." Dexter took a deep breath. He took another. "Helium?"

He closed his eyes and grimaced as he waited to see if Mrs. Pinkerton would allow that answer.

Mrs. Pinkerton paused. "Correct."

Dexter nearly fainted.

"Next?"

"Beryllium."

Sarah smacked her hand on her face. "Lithium," she muttered. "Lithium!"

"I mean lithium," Dexter said.

Mrs. Pinkerton let out an inhuman growl and Jacob saw purple veins popping out on her face in places he didn't even know people had veins. She grasped her ruler and broke it over her knee, flinging the pieces up

in the air. "Cheating?! In my classroom?" She rushed toward Dexter, who shrunk away in fear.

Jacob sprang into action. No one bullied Dexter, especially not a substitute teacher. It was time for the nuclear option.

He reached into his desk and pulled out a baseball he had hidden away in case of emergency. He had practiced for hours for just this occasion. He threw the baseball toward the ceiling and hit the emergency fire sprinkler, which immediately burst into pieces and began drenching the class with heavy streams of water.

The entire class screamed and began a mad rush toward the door, overturning desks and chairs and slipping in the water. Sarah laughed hysterically and slapped Jacob on the back.

Amid the pandemonium, Dexter backed up against the wall and accidentally knocked a large framed picture of Albert Einstein to the ground, which then tipped over and bumped Miss Banks's rolling chair, which rolled just far enough so that the arm of the chair barely clipped Mrs. Pinkerton's coffee mug, which slid off of the desk, fell ever so slowly, crashed, and shattered on the floor into a million pieces.

As the class streamed into the hallway and as water rained down, Jacob, Sarah, and Dexter stared at Mrs.

Pinkerton, who looked completely calm. It was almost as if her "Reach for the Stars" coffee mug had not just been destroyed and she was not being doused with water at the rate of two gallons per second. In fact, she acted as if it were the most natural thing in the universe.

"Dexter Goldstein, Sarah Daisy, Jacob Wonderbar. Principal's office. Now."

"But—" all three said at once.

"NOW."

CHAPTER 2

First things first," Mr. Bradley, the principal of Magellan Middle School, said to Jacob, Dexter, and Sarah as they sat soaking wet in his office, hoping they would not be in too much trouble. "You're in a great deal of trouble. Coffee mugs exploding, classrooms flooding, allegations of cheating, an angry substitute teacher. This is all quite serious. Punishment will be leveled."

Mr. Bradley was completely bald except for a small patch of hair near the base of his neck that had somehow managed to avoid the catastrophic fate of the rest of the hair population on his head. His black glasses made his eyes appear approximately three times larger than they actually were, although his eyes were plenty big to begin with. He wore a yellowing white shirt and a red tie spotted with toothpaste. It's best that his mustache not be mentioned at all.

Mr. Bradley tapped his forehead in thought. "Considering the facts at hand, Sarah Daisy, you may return to the classroom. You are clearly innocent."

"What? But I'm the one who started this whole thing when I blurted out the answer. It's my fault!"

Mr. Bradley shook his head. "You don't understand. You couldn't possibly be guilty."

Sarah closed her eyes and let out a long exhale of pure resignation. She clenched her hands into fists. "It's because I'm a cute little girl, isn't it?"

"Yes! Yes, I would say that is precisely it," Mr. Bradley said.

"This is discrimination! What if I wasn't a girl? What if I had warts all over my face? Would you still treat me like a silly little girl? This is horrible! I demand equal punishment."

Mr. Bradley laughed and clapped his hands. "Such a clever girl. Back to class with you."

Sarah Daisy stormed out of the office, slamming the door as she left.

"Dexter Goldstein . . . Dexter Goldstein . . . what shall we do with you? Mr. Wonderbar's favorite accomplice, if I'm not mistaken, and I'm never mistaken. What say you?"

Jacob waited for Dexter to defend himself since he had only broken Mrs. Pinkerton's mug by accident and was otherwise completely blameless.

Instead, Dexter ran his hand through his hair, sighed, and said, "Nothing. I'm guilty as charged." He looked over at Jacob. "Again."

Jacob knew why Dexter had issued a false confession. He had gotten Dexter into enough trouble that adults very rarely believed either of them when they claimed to be innocent. Mr. Bradley didn't believe them when they said they weren't the ones who taped the words "in the bathroom" onto all of Ms. Franklin's inspirational posters celebrating qualities like determination and creativity, and he certainly wouldn't believe that a flooded classroom was Jacob Wonderbar's sole responsibility. After their many successful pranks over the past couple of years, Dexter's only hope in the face of punishment was to admit guilt and hope for leniency. Even when he wasn't actually at fault.

Mr. Bradley adjusted some of the souvenirs that littered his desk, including a clock in the shape of an old sailing ship and a gold star that said "#1 Principal." He took out a pen, scribbled on a piece of paper, tore it off of his tablet, carefully folded it, and handed it over to Dexter.

Dexter opened it very slowly. It read: "I am giving you two hours of detention. Your punishment will be halved if you answer this question correctly: Who is your favorite principal?"

"Um. You are?" Dexter said.

"Correct! I knew I could count on you. You may return to class. I will see you in detention next Wednesday."

Dexter sat still for a few seconds. "My mom is going to kill me," he whispered. Then he stood up, punched Jacob lightly on the shoulder, and left Jacob and Mr. Bradley staring at each other in silence. Mr. Bradley scratched his mustache and cleared his throat.

"Well well, Mr. Wonderbar, we meet again. I would say it's a pleasure, only it's not. So many office visits this year. Disruptions, lack of focus, practical jokes . . . you are a regular criminal mastermind. Do you know what your teacher Miss Banks said about you the other day?"

Jacob shook his head.

"She said that you show a great deal of promise. Did you know that? I strenuously disagreed with her, of course."

Jacob thought about the time he let the air out of Miss Banks's bike tires and was mystified that she had said something nice about him in private.

"But no matter. Today we have a case where you have soaked a thoroughly distressed Mrs. Pinkerton. A priceless coffee mug has been destroyed. I don't know that there are enough hours in the day to give you the detention you deserve. What is your mother going to think about all of this?"

Jacob stood up out of his seat. "I do not repent!"

Mr. Bradley took off his glasses and rubbed his eyes.

"Mr. Bradley. Rather than locking us up in detention, wouldn't your time be better served reconsidering your policy for hiring substitute teachers? Didn't you at least do a background check on that woman? We could have all been killed! How could I be punished for saving the class from a crazy person? I should probably receive a medal. There's no need to call my mom."

Mr. Bradley wiped his glasses with his tie and put them back on. "I'm not going to call your mother."

"Whew."

"That would be redundant. We spoke just before you came into my office. A preemptive strike, they call it."

"What?!"

"She'll be here in two minutes."

CHAPTER 3

Jacob stepped carefully into his mom's hybrid SUV and shut the door. He could tell that she had been in a meeting because she was driving without a shoe on her right foot, which meant she had been wearing high heels, which meant an especially important meeting.

Jacob wasn't exactly sure what his mom did at work. It had something to do with people trading gasoline, only it wasn't gasoline you could buy at a gas station, it was sort of like gasoline you could buy in the future. They didn't have a bunch of barrels of oil in their garage or anything like that; it was all done on computers. When people asked his mom what she did for a living, she said "commodity futures trading," but Jacob could tell that most adults didn't really know what that meant either.

It was silent in the car, and Jacob couldn't bear it. He said quickly, "I know. You don't want to say anything you'll regret later. I understand."

Jacob's mom didn't say anything, and he wondered what unspeakable thoughts were running through her mind. He knew from past experience that he had a fifteen-minute reprieve until they arrived home and she had calmed herself down enough to lecture him with a reasonably level head. He started mentally outlining his opening statement.

"Then why am I here picking you up at school?" she said. "What am I supposed to do? I can't drop everything at work every time you act up in class."

Jacob froze. It was a surprise attack. He had no choice but to opt for complete denial. "Mom! This one wasn't my fault!"

Based on the skeptical look on her face, Jacob knew that his mom was remembering the last time Jacob had insisted that a visit with Mr. Bradley wasn't his fault. That incident had involved a great deal of glue, a handful of feathers, and a teacher's bottom, and had been, in fact, 100 percent completely Jacob's fault.

"Okay," Jacob said, "that time with the feathers was me. But this time I'm innocent!"

"Jacob . . ." his mom began.

"No, I'm serious! This time it was Sarah and Dexter. I promise."

"I don't believe you."

"Mom!"

"How am I supposed to believe you, Jacob? Honestly. After the last two years of you acting up and getting into trouble at least once a week, tell me, why would I believe you when you say an incident at school isn't your fault? I've had to replace three sprinklers in the backyard because you 'accidentally' hit them with your baseball. Are you also going to try and tell me you weren't using them for target practice?"

Jacob leaned back in his seat. She had played her hand well. It was wildly improbable that anyone but him could have destroyed a fire sprinkler with a well-aimed baseball in order to douse an evil substitute.

"Did you or did you not promise that you would stop getting into trouble?"

He nodded solemnly. "That is a fair question."

Jacob's mom pursed her lips together, but then she smiled despite herself. "Listen to you. You know, sometimes you take after your father a little too much for your own good."

Jacob turned away and looked out the window. He

picked at the plastic on the door handle. "I don't want to talk about that person."

Jacob's mom stopped the car, reached over, and placed her hand on his shoulder. "Jacob, I'm sorry. That was a loaded thing to say."

He kept staring out the window and wondered if his mom knew how much he thought about his dad since he had moved to Milwaukee. "I don't want to be anything like him."

"Well, the good thing about the world is that you can be whoever you want to be. You don't have to be like your father. But until you're eighteen years old you will follow my rules."

Jacob's mom suddenly clenched his shoulder and made him look her in the eye. "Listen to me carefully," she said. "This is the last time you will get into trouble and I mean that very sincerely. You are officially not allowed to have any fun until I say you can have fun again, which will most likely be around the time you have forgotten what having fun even feels like. Do you understand me?"

Jacob thought about protesting further, but he accepted his punishment with a nod.

CHAPTER 4

Jacob and his mom lived in a subdivision where all of the houses were constructed from one of three designs that everyone chose from a brochure when the subdivision was still a scrubby field, but when the houses were built they all ended up looking pretty much the same. Jacob's house had a garage facing the street, a brown door set back a little bit from that, and a second story with shutters around the windows and a flat roof. The only way you could tell Jacob's house from Sarah's and Dexter's houses down the street was that Dexter's shutters were red and Sarah's shutters were dark green. Jacob's were also dark green, but his house had a faded wreath with fake flowers on the door. Sometimes when Jacob was at Dexter's house he would try to put his trash under the sink without remembering that Dexter's parents kept the trash in a bin next to the counter. Other than that, the inside of their houses were basically the same too.

He took the garbage out to the curb and saw the first firefly of the year. He watched it flicker off and on and he sat down on the grass for a moment to see where it would fly. Summer was coming, the night had just a hint of mugginess to it, and the moon was a brilliant orange, which Jacob knew was probably because of pollution in the atmosphere, but at that moment he didn't mind because it looked amazing. He thought about his dad and wondered what he was doing that night, and if he might be outside looking at the moon as well, maybe even thinking about Jacob.

He stared at his hands, a soft brown color that was lighter than his mom's dark skin and darker than his dad's light skin. It was proof that he was half of his mom and half of his dad, but since he didn't look like either of them, it also made him something else entirely. Ever since his dad had left he felt like he only knew half of himself. The only tangible reminder that he'd once had a dad was his lighter skin.

He saw some kids approaching down the street and recognized the forms of Dexter and Sarah. When Jacob saw Sarah outside he remembered that it was the second Tuesday of the month, since Mondays she had ballet rehearsal and Wednesdays she had piano practice and Thursdays she had study hall, where her parents assigned extra non-school essays on things like the Gadsden Purchase and the Brandenburg Concertos and other things Jacob knew nothing about. Friday night was family movie night with her parents and her little sister, weekends were reserved for soccer, and during summer vacation her parents took her all around the country to visit colleges and museums. She had Mandarin lessons every other Tuesday, and since it was an odd-numbered month that meant she had the evenings of the second and fourth Tuesdays set aside as friend time, assuming she had finished her homework and any possible extra credit, only this month she had a big piano recital on the fourth Tuesday, which meant it was definitely the second Tuesday, and the only day Jacob, Dexter, and Sarah would be able to spend time together after school all month.

Their tradition of hanging out whenever Sarah had a free night had begun after Jacob's dad had left a few years back. After a week cooped up in his house alone Jacob had asked them to go into the forest down the street to make a pact. When they reached their favorite clearing, Jacob had raised the stick he was carrying and proposed that they be blood friends. Dexter had looked at his hand and said, "No offense, but I'm not cutting myself. I'd probably get gangrene or something."

Jacob traced a circle in the dirt with his stick and agreed he wasn't very interested in cutting himself either, and in the end they decided to swear on the stars that they would always be there for one another no matter what, with a bond that was stronger than best friends. Then they high-fived and threw some rocks around the clearing before hearing a noise that made them run out of the forest laughing because they were scared raccoons were after them.

Since that time, Sarah's parents forced her to join more and more extracurriculars, and their nights together had dwindled down to maybe once or twice a month depending on Sarah's schedule.

"Nice work, Jake," Sarah called out as they approached Jacob's lawn. Sarah was the only person Jacob let call him Jake. "We got to spend the rest of the day in the gym playing dodgeball. It was like we were in third grade all over again."

"Really?" Jacob imagined the backslaps and congratulations he would receive when he returned to school. Usually when he forced a substitute to flee, the class would have to read silently for the rest of the day with Principal Bradley, which was almost worse than having a sub. Giving his class the gift of dodgeball nearly made up for the fact that he was grounded.

"Yeah, it was great. Oh, also, Dexter almost got beat up by the MacKenzie twins on the way home."

Jacob's jaw clenched. The MacKenzies must have known that he would be stuck at home, unable to extend his customary Dexter protection. "What happened?"

"They had him cornered by the basketball hoop, but I jumped in front of them and said that I would eat their eyeballs for breakfast if they so much as laid a finger on him. I think they believed me."

Jacob smiled at Dexter. "She saved you?"

Dexter shifted on his feet and looked away. "It wasn't a proud moment."

"So what about you, Jake? What's the punishment?"

"Ugh. My mom was so mad, she said—"

Suddenly the street lit up and there was a flash in the forest, almost like an explosion without a sound. A green laser shot up into the sky and then disappeared just as quickly. A moment later there was a faint whirring noise and a hiss. Then the street was silent again.

"Whoa," Dexter said.

Jacob's heart raced. Strange things did not tend to happen on their street. They always happened on other, more exciting streets that he saw on the news.

"What in the heck was that?" Sarah asked.

They watched and listened to see if any more strange lights or noises came from the forest, but nothing more happened.

"Maybe someone should check it out?" Dexter asked. He sat down on the curb.

Jacob pondered whether investigating a strange light in the forest fell under his mom's general prohibition against having fun. While he would certainly find the experience exhilarating, he didn't know if it could be considered "fun" per se, since danger should be confronted only with the utmost seriousness, and serious was the opposite of fun. He concluded that the activity fell under the category "protecting the neighborhood."

"I'll check it out," Jacob said.

"I'm coming with you," Sarah said.

Jacob held up his hand. "No, I've got this."

"Jake . . ."

"Keep Dexter company," he said.

Dexter nodded eagerly. "I actually wouldn't mind some company."

Sarah kicked the ground and said, "Fine." She sat down next to Dexter in a huff.

Jacob walked slowly toward the end of the block, turned to give one last wave to Sarah and Dexter, and stepped into the forest. The bright moon cast strange shadows all around him. He hadn't ever ventured into the woods alone after dark. He swallowed, steadied his nerves, and walked farther in.

He pushed past the thorny bushes and ducked under low branches, listening carefully for strange noises. When he had nearly reached the clearing, he heard a twig snap. He stopped.

He saw a tall man. Jacob crouched behind a bush and watched him as his heart pounded in his chest. The man had silver hair and was dressed head to toe in . . . silver. Jacob pieced together more details. Shoes? Silver boots. Pants? Silver. Skin? Very light, but essentially silver. The moon seemed to reflect off every part of him. Jacob wondered if he could take on an old silver man if it came down to a fight.

The man turned to Jacob and they locked eyes. His eyes were not actually silver, but rather a more normal brown.

Jacob tensed.

"There you are," the man said. "Do you know where I can get a corndog?"

CHAPTER 5

The silver man stood patiently on the sidewalk while Jacob, Sarah, and Dexter considered his offer.

"A corndog for a spaceship?" Sarah asked. "You're crazy."

"Glad to be rid of it," the man said. "That thing has a serious attitude problem."

Sarah narrowed her eyes suspiciously. Jacob had to admit that he had some major doubts that the man in silver would trade them a spaceship for a corndog, which, while obviously quite delicious, could be obtained easily on Earth. He wondered if it was a trap.

"Prove to us that you're not from Earth," Jacob said.

The man said in a high-pitched voice, "Hi! I'm a bird! How are you?"

"What does that prove?" Sarah asked.

The man looked at Sarah like she was crazy. "That's what the birds sound like on my planet."

"Ugh," Sarah said. "He probably painted a box and left it in the forest or something."

"I've got it!" Dexter shouted, suddenly excited. "You have chosen us out of all of the people in the entire universe to take your spaceship! It's our destiny!"

The silver man shook his head. "No. I picked this town at random."

"Oh," Dexter said. "Wait. I know. The galaxy is in trouble and we're the only ones who can save it!"

"The galaxy is fine."

"Do we have secret powers?"

"Not that I know of."

Everyone stood there for a few more seconds in silence.

"About that corndog . . ." the silver man said.

He took out a set of jagged keys and dangled them. Sarah reached for them, but the man snatched them away again and put them in his pocket.

Jacob shrugged. "I'm pretty sure we have some corndogs in the freezer. What do you guys think?"

Sarah leaned forward and gave the silver man a fierce scowl. "I guess it wouldn't cost us much if he's lying."

Jacob went inside to microwave a corndog while Dexter and Sarah stood on the sidewalk with the silver man.

"So . . . What planet are you from exactly?" Dexter asked.

"You wouldn't have heard of it."

"Oh. Do you know someone from your planet named Mr. Bradley?" Dexter asked. "He's bald."

"Who?"

"Never mind."

After a couple of minutes of awkward silence, Jacob came back out with a corndog on a paper plate with some ketchup. "Sorry it took so long. I had to explain to my mom why I needed more food after eating a whole plate of tuna surprise, then she accused me of throwing away my dinner when she wasn't watching. But she went upstairs to go look at what the Asian stock markets are doing, so I think I'm safe for a few minutes. Anyway, here's your corndog."

The silver man tossed the keys to Jacob, grabbed the plate, and started walking down the street. "See ya."

"Wait," Sarah said, "how do we—"

"You'll figure it out."

The trio watched the silver man walk down the sidewalk and disappear around the corner.

CHAPTER 6

They found the spaceship sitting peacefully in a clearing in the forest, reflecting the orange moonlight. It was majestic, a giant antique contraption made out of old copper steam pipes and stainless steel plating with tubes twisting and turning around the outside. It was shaped like a big piece of pie, with a slightly tarnished mirrored cockpit bumping out on top and an entryway with steps lowering down to the ground at the back where the crust would have been. The spaceship looked like it was resting on some crushed shrubs and saplings, but Jacob realized instead it was somehow hovering above the forest floor and was barely bending some of the larger trees, which couldn't have appreciated the sudden appearance of an otherworldly, hovering, shiny, triangle-shaped vessel from another planet.

After staring at it with their jaws in various states of slackness, it wasn't very long before Jacob, Dexter, and Sarah began arguing about what they should do with it.

"What good is a spaceship if you don't fly around in it?" Jacob asked.

"There is no way I'm getting inside that thing," Dexter said.

"Jake, do you have any idea what my parents would do to me if they found out I was cavorting around in outer space?" Sarah asked.

"My parents would probably say they were disappointed in me, in that voice they use when they're disappointed in me," Dexter said, shaking his head. "I really hate the disappointed voice."

"Forget having any time to hang out with you guys," Sarah said. "My parents would probably make me take oboe lessons or something."

Jacob raised his hands and appealed for calm. "Guys. We're arguing about a spaceship. A *spaceship*. I mean, just look at it."

They turned and looked at the spaceship. Its metal gleamed and its hatch beckoned with soft yellow light.

"It is kind of amazing," Sarah said, stepping toward it.

"I can't wait any longer," Jacob said. He started running for the entrance.

"Guys, I really shouldn't," Dexter said with a slight tremor in his voice.

Jacob stopped in his tracks. He had heard Dexter say "Guys, I really shouldn't" many times. It was inevitably followed by him muttering, "Yeah, I should probably be going now" and running off toward home before anyone could stop him. Jacob knew that if there was anything that Dexter needed, it was a little more fun in his life. The Goldsteins' idea of a good time was eating organic granola bars and rearranging their closets.

"Come on, Dexter," Jacob said. "You don't want to get old and look back on your life and think, 'Wow, if only I had looked inside that spaceship that magically appeared on my street. Maybe I should have checked that thing out.' Don't be so scared."

Dexter rubbed the heels of his palms together. "I'm not scared," he said. "It's just that . . . What if there's a law against underage space driving?"

"I promise there's no law against underage space driving."

"But what about—"

"You're coming with us. Don't be a chicken."

Dexter finally said, "I guess it wouldn't hurt to at least look at the inside."

Jacob scrambled up the ladder and gasped when he stepped inside the belly of the spaceship. Instead of the futuristic metal and plastic he had been expecting, it was almost as if they had stepped back in time onto an old pirate ship. The walls and ceiling of the ship were covered in a rich mahogany, the floor was made of rough-hewn planks, and in the middle stood a proud, ornate circular staircase with a pearl banister that led to the cockpit.

Four doors opened up off of the hold, and the children each headed for a different one.

Dexter reached his door first and threw it open. The room was filled with huge wooden casks and some fearsome weaponry that he would need to hide from Jacob. "Supply room," he called out to the others.

Jacob reached his room next and stepped inside. Two very inviting hammocks hung from the ceiling, and there were a few cast-iron trunks on the floor. "Sleeping quarters," he yelled.

Sarah headed straight to the big door in the front of the ship, and when she opened it she simply yelled, "Dibs! Dibs dibs dibs dibs dibs dibs dibs!!"

Jacob and Dexter came rushing in and saw the magnificent captain's quarters that Sarah had claimed for her own. The room comprised the front wedge of the ship, and beautiful rectangular windows looked out on the moonlit forest. Jacob could only imagine what the view would be like when they reached outer space. The parts of the walls that were not windowed were covered by old space-faring maps printed on yellowing paper. A large wooden armoire stood in one corner next to a large desk. But what had captured Sarah's attention was a massive four-post bed with an alien mermaid carved into the headboard. The bed was covered in soft, billowy comforters, and Sarah had already sprawled across them.

"Can someone fetch me a spot of tea?" she called out. "Ha-ha! Don't even think you can talk me out of this room, Jake. I'll fight you to the death."

Dexter went out and threw open the fourth door, hoping to find the most spectacular room of all, but instead he found a toilet and shower. "Oh. Bathroom," he said.

Jacob's eyes widened. "Wait. What about the cockpit?"

Jacob and Dexter raced up the circular staircase. The cockpit was covered with a glass dome, which allowed a view all around the ship. Two big seats sat forward in the front with a steering wheel for each side. An impressive array of wooden knobs and metal levers surrounded both seats. Two more seats sat back behind, with still more knobs, levers, pulleys, and buttons. Dexter made a beeline for one of the rear seats and plopped down. "There is no way I'm driving this thing."

Jacob went and sat in the larger captain's chair, and when Sarah reached the cockpit she pressed her lips together. "You think I can't drive a spaceship?" she muttered.

"I got here first! He gave me the keys. Please?" Jacob adopted his best pleading face, which didn't often sway the sympathies of Sarah Daisy, but on this occasion he had to try. He was reasonably sure he would be the first sixth grader ever to blast off into space, and he imagined that it would result in a great deal of fame. If he was listed in a history book he might even be inclined to read one someday.

Sarah frowned. "Fine. It's your lucky day after all." She joined him at the front in the first mate's seat.

Jacob found the ignition, inserted the biggest key, and turned it. The spaceship gave a satisfying hum. He turned to Sarah and said, "So where do you guys want to—"

Jacob didn't have a chance to finish the question. The spaceship had already blasted off.

CHAPTER 7

There goes Mars!" Dexter shouted as the red planet rushed past the window.

The spaceship was speeding through the solar system at an impressive velocity. Jacob and Sarah furiously spun the wheels and pushed every button they could find, but nothing was changing the ship's course. All of the buttons were labeled with otherworldly letters that they couldn't read.

"What's going on?" Jacob yelled.

"Asteroid belt!" Dexter called out.

"I think we're going faster!" Sarah shouted.

Jacob knew he was in trouble. The ship wasn't slowing down, and Earth was a tiny dot in the rearview monitor. He had thought they would just fly to space and back, or maybe buzz Hong Kong. He hadn't even considered that they would zoom past planets and leave Earth far behind.

"Jupiter!" Dexter yelled.

"You don't have to yell so loud," Sarah said.

"I'm very excited!" Dexter yelled.

The huge planet loomed with its red dot, and they could see the swirling clouds in the atmosphere.

After pushing just about every button in the cabin, Jacob saw one with an image of a tongue on it, and he pressed it. Suddenly all of the buttons changed to another language, and the letters looked a little closer to an Earth language.

"Those were simplified Chinese characters!" Sarah said.

Jacob kept pressing the button, and finally the labels switched over to English. But Jacob was pressing the button so frantically he accidentally pressed it one extra time, and the buttons became unreadable again.

"Oops," Jacob said.

"Saturn!" Dexter yelled.

Jacob looked out the cockpit window. They were so close to Saturn, he could see huge chunks of ice within its rings, reflecting the increasingly faraway sun. A few small white moons stood out in the darkness of space.

"Wow," Dexter said.

"No time," Sarah said. "Jake, are you going to stop this thing or what?"

"This is really bad!" Dexter shouted. "Oh, there goes . . . Um . . . Which one is that again?"

"Uranus," Sarah said.

"Uranus!" Dexter yelled.

Jacob kept pressing the tongue button, and after pressing it more than a hundred times it finally switched to English, but at that point he was so used to pressing the button, he pushed past it again, and the buttons switched back to an unreadable language.

"No!" Jacob smacked his hand on his head. "English! English!"

The buttons all switched to English.

"Oh," Jacob said.

"Neptune!" Dexter yelled.

Sarah was scratching her head. "Something's not right here. The planets in the solar system aren't all just lined up in a row, they're scattered all over in their orbits. But the spaceship is taking us right to each of them in order. Are we on some sort of tour? And Jake, are you going to get control of this ship?"

"Pluto!" Dexter yelled.

Jacob quickly found the button that said "Override," and with a lurch he found himself at the wheel of a spaceship that was rocketing through the galaxy and quickly leaving the solar system behind. A small planet whizzed by outside the window.

"That's . . . I'm not sure what that was!" Dexter said.

The spaceship swung wildly around as Jacob tried to gauge the sensitivity of the wheel, and yet their speed was only increasing. The rest of the Milky Way galaxy loomed ahead, a soft white streak across the sky, and one large star in particular that happened to be growing larger and larger in the window as the ship sped toward it.

"Jake, look, look!"

"I see it!" Jacob said.

The star was now so bright that Jacob imagined he could feel the heat, but the ship still felt cool on the inside. Jacob didn't yet know how to hit the brakes, so he did the only thing he could think to do: He spun the wheel as fast as he could.

The ship quickly arced to the right, and a new problem came into view.

"Big random planet!" Dexter yelled.

A massive gray pockmarked planet, completely barren and dusty, loomed straight ahead. They were on a collision course and he didn't think he'd be able to turn away in time. Jacob scanned the console for options. He saw a button that said "Huge missile launcher."

"I'm going to shoot it with a missile."

"Jake, what if there are aliens on that planet?!" Sarah said.

"No choice!"

"Hurry!" Dexter said.

Jacob quickly pressed the button and the ship shuddered as two missiles darted ahead straight toward the planet. They landed with a spectacular explosion and sent the planet careening out of their path. Jacob pressed another button that said "Elliptical slingshot," and the ship sped forward, swung a tight orbit around the planet, and used the gravity to shoot off in another direction like a slingshot. The trio looked out the window as the planet hurtled toward the star.

Jacob, Sarah, and Dexter watched the space carnage as their ship raced away. The planet collided into the star with a spectacular blast of white light. It exploded into another star, creating a still larger explosion, and then another, and another, and still yet another and another, brighter and brighter, and as they sped rapidly away, what had once been a light smattering of stars in the distance looked like a streak of spilled milk

across the sky.

Jacob finally found the brakes and stopped the spaceship. They sat in space, watching exploding stars and
an unfolding problem of cosmic proportions.

Stars had exploded. Planets had been obliterated.
The sky was streaked with star guts. Jacob, Dexter,
and Sarah looked at one another in stunned silence.

"I think we just broke the universe," Dexter said.

CHAPTER 8

The explosions seemed to have stopped, but space was still very bright in the aftermath of the big kapow, and a giant streak of white across the sky sometimes pulsated as the stars settled into a messy new arrangement that Dexter dubbed the Spilled Milky Way galaxy. Jacob ran his hands over his face. The first planet had looked deserted, but he hoped there weren't any people or aliens or strange men dressed in silver who lived on any of the other planets they had just destroyed.

"Well?" Sarah asked. "What are we going to do?"

Dexter raised his hand.

Sarah said, "Um. Dexter?"

"It's time to go home," he said. "Think about how worried our parents are right now. We've been gone at least an hour, and who knows how long it's going to take us to get back to Earth."

Sarah said, "Dexter's right. It's time to go home, Jake."

They turned to Jacob, waiting for his agreement. He thought about his mom and how she must have finished checking the stock markets. She might have even wandered downstairs and realized he was missing. Given the day's events she probably thought he had run away, and since his mom was not the most composed individual in a crisis, Jacob imagined that the entire neighborhood was currently feeling the formidable wrath of her panic. But then he shook his worried mom out of his head. He had pressing space matters to attend to. He pointed at the cockpit window. "I'm not going home until I've spacewalked."

Sarah looked quickly over at Dexter, waiting for his reaction. A slow grin spread across his face.

They jumped up and went scrambling down the staircase and into the hold. "Spacesuits!" Dexter shouted. "We must have spacesuits!"

Jacob ran into the supply room and saw a huge assortment of space blasters, projectile launchers, and some devilish devices whose purpose he couldn't even begin to imagine. Dexter and Sarah caught up with him and saw the ideas that were clearly forming in

Jacob's head. "I was kind of hoping you wouldn't see those," Dexter said.

They went rooting through the bins and found plenty of food and supplies, but no spacesuits.

Jacob ran out of the supply room and into his bunk. He threw open the metal trunk. "Jackpot!"

He pulled out a spacesuit. It was made of a lightweight material that gave off a soft glow, and was entirely silver except for a white triangle on the chest and orange bands around the shoulders. He also found a clear helmet, orange gloves and boots, and a small gray jetpack that attached with an orange belt. "Here we go!" he said.

Dexter ran in, saw Jacob's spacesuit, and opened the other trunk. "My boots are green!"

They ran into the captain's room with Sarah, who threw open the great armoire, and said, "Oh, you gotta be kidding me."

She pulled out her boots and showed them to Jacob and Dexter.

"What?" Jacob asked. "They're purple."

"They're *lavender!*" she shouted. "Oh, sure, give the girl the lavender boots. I'm trading. One of you has to give me your boots."

Jacob and Dexter ran out of the room to go put on their spacesuits.

"This is so sexist!" Sarah yelled after them.

Dexter and Jacob quickly put on their spacesuits and waited for Sarah. When she emerged from the captain's quarters wearing her spacesuit she shook her head. "Don't you think it's a little bit strange that there were spacesuits that just happened to fit us already on board this ship? In the same rooms we chose? Did someone plan this trip for us?"

Jacob ran over to the rear of the hold and found the exit button. "Yes, it's very strange. In fact, let's talk about it some more. In *outer space*."

He pressed the button. The rear door opened with a hiss, and Jacob dove out into space.

Dexter stepped over to the edge and watched Jacob sail around, twisting and turning in loops and doing a series of awkward somersaults in zero gravity.

Sarah dove out right after Jacob, and Dexter gingerly stepped out and felt the outer space vacuum pull him away from the ship.

Jacob quickly figured out that his spacesuit and jetpack had a self-propulsion system. When he put his hands forward like he was diving into water, he zoomed forward. Every lean sent him in a different direction, and all he had to do was put his hands to his side to hit the brakes. He zoomed in a straight line away from the spaceship before doubling back in a graceful arc.

"This is pretty much the coolest thing ever," Jacob said through the intercom.

"I would have to agree," Sarah said after doing a perfect figure eight.

Dexter was just drifting in space by himself and not making any sudden movements. "I think I'm getting space sick."

Jacob marveled that he was spacewalking with his favorite people from Earth, floating around and doing flips and seeing what zero gravity really felt like: kind of like swimming, only waving your arms and kicking your legs didn't get you very far.

Jacob went zooming after Sarah and gave her leg a strong shove, which sent her careening in circles. She righted course and charged straight for Jacob's stomach, slamming into him with her shoulder. "Oof," Jacob said, doubling over.

He grabbed her by the shoulders, and Sarah and Jacob made eye contact, floating together slowly. Sarah smiled. Then she gave him a fierce head butt, helmet to helmet.

"Ow!"

"Ha-ha!"

Jacob flew away in the opposite direction.

That was when he saw the lights of the police cruiser.

CHAPTER 9

Two policemen with bright pink skin emerged from a sleek police space cruiser striped with blue and black bars. The officers wore dark blue spacesuits that barely contained their massive bodies, and they looked as if they were pumped full of air to the bursting point. As they ushered the children back onto the man in silver's spaceship, Jacob realized he was probably in violation of a surprisingly vast array of interplanetary laws. Now that he knew there really were humans in outer space, he wondered if the planets they had destroyed had actually been inhabited. He leaned over and put his face in his hands.

The two space officers introduced themselves as Officers Bosendorfer and Erard.

"First question," Officer Bosendorfer said, "who is

responsible for this disaster?"

"I—" Jacob said.

"Not you," Officer Erard said.

Sarah and Dexter shook their heads.

"You either," Officer Erard said.

Jacob heard a pained sigh, and a sassy female voice said, "I was giving these children a perfectly good and incredibly fast tour of their star system when they decided to override my systems and managed to destroy a very nice planet and several star systems. It's been simply ghastly."

Sarah gasped. "The spaceship can talk?"

"What did you expect?" she said.

"Why didn't you tell us?" Sarah asked.

The ship sighed again. "I am so bored right now."

Officers Bosendorfer and Erard gave each other meaningful glances. "Children, this next question is quite serious. What rank are you in the Earther army that has been sent to destroy Astrals once and for all?"

"Generals at least, by the looks of them," Officer Erard whispered to Officer Bosendorfer.

"We are peace-loving people," Officer Bosendorfer said, holding up his hands. "We just want to enjoy life. We know that by age twelve most Earther children have already served in several wars, but we don't want to fight with you."

Jacob looked at Sarah, who shook her head with her eyes wide. "What's an Astral?" Jacob asked.

Officer Bosendorfer snorted. "Young man, we are not that easily fooled. Please answer the question. Are you generals or is one of you the Earther leader?"

"Um," Sarah said. "That whole space kapow thing was an accident! We didn't do it on purpose. This isn't a war."

Officer Bosendorfer looked at Sarah as if she were speaking nonsense, but Officer Erard said cautiously, "Young lady, are you telling us the truth?"

"It was an accident!" Sarah shouted.

Officer Bosendorfer slumped into his chair in relief. "Oh, thank the universe. I'm too lazy to fight a war."

Jacob turned back and looked at the Spilled Milky Way galaxy, still flashing with explosions. "What about those planets?" he asked quietly. "What did we do?"

Officers Bosendorfer and Erard turned to look at the space kapow. "Oh. Yes. While apparently it was not an act of intergalactic war, you children made quite a serious mess."

Jacob's chest tightened as he readied himself for charges against outer space humanity.

Officers Bosendorfer and Erard nodded to each other. "And after painstaking deliberation we will let you kids off with a warning. You're very fortunate those planets were very ugly and uninhabitable. You're also lucky that Officer Erard and I have a powerful aversion to paperwork."

"Overpowering," Officer Erard agreed.

Jacob felt like he could breathe again.

"Now we can go home!" Dexter said.

Officer Erard tapped his head with his finger. "Now hold on there. Aren't you from Earth?" he asked.

"Yes," he said.

"That's what I thought." Officer Erard nodded. "You can't go home."

"What?!" Sarah shrieked.

"Why not?" Jacob asked.

Officers Bosendorfer and Erard peered at the children as if they were quite dim. "Because you broke the universe," Officer Bosendorfer said. He pointed out the window at the white smear across the sky. "You can't very well fly through that. That is the way to Earth."

All the blood in Jacob's face rushed in the direction of his space boots as it dawned on him that they could be stuck in space for a very long time. He could scarcely imagine the creative, sadistic measures of grounding his mother would employ upon his return. She would take away fun things he never knew he appreciated. She might even invent fun things that had never before existed only to deny Jacob the pleasure of participating in them. He didn't even have a way of telling her they were still alive. Of course, that assumed that the space kapow didn't also . . .

"Is Earth okay?" Jacob asked quickly. "We didn't destroy that too, did we?"

Officer Erard looked at his handheld computer. "It's probably fine."

"Probably?!" Dexter cried.

"Couldn't really say. The important thing is that no Astral colonies were destroyed."

Dexter wiped his face with his hands and tried to

use his words. "Could we . . . go . . . around the . . . uh . . . Spilled Milky Way galaxy? To make sure . . . our planet is still there?"

Officer Erard waved his hand vaguely. "Radiation."

"That sounds bad!" Sarah shrieked.

"But don't worry," Officer Bosendorfer said cheerfully. "These things usually clear up in a couple thousand years."

Dexter had a sudden coughing fit.

Officer Erard's handheld device squawked to life. "Officer Bosendorfer and Officer Erard, come in. Officer Bosendorfer and Officer Erard, come in. Please respond immediately to a code brown."

Suddenly it was Officers Bosendorfer's and Erard's turn to look pale. Officer Erard gasped for breath. "Do you . . . do you mean . . ."

"Mick Cracken is headed your way. You must give chase!"

"Mick Cracken?!" Officer Bosendorfer shuddered. His bottom lip began to quiver and he looked as if he might cry. "Do we have to?"

CHAPTER 10

Jacob had read that outer space is completely silent because there's no air or water or anything else to transmit sound, just one big vacuum of nothing. That didn't apply to the insides of spaceships, of course, because they were filled with air, but still, Jacob never would have guessed that the quietest moment he would experience in outer space would have involved two space officers stunned into silence by the name Mick Cracken.

Officers Bosendorfer and Erard were slumped in their chairs staring out the cockpit window, radiating an acute sense of panic. Officer Bosendorfer sniffed once and rubbed his eyes. Officer Erard stared straight up at the roof and shook his head. Jacob, Sarah, and Dexter looked around at one another and shrugged their shoulders.

Finally, Sarah Daisy broke the quiet. "Who's Mick Cracken?"

Officer Bosendorfer waved his hand at her. "Young lady, this is no time for bravery," he said.

Officer Erard sighed. "You know I can't even say his name?"

"I can say his name," Officer Bosendorfer said. "But it makes me shudder every time. Watch this. Mick Cracken." Officer Bosendorfer didn't shudder. "Well, that time I didn't shudder, but usually I shudder. It's not usually something I can control, I . . ." Officer Bosendorfer shuddered. "Oh. There. See? Delayed shudder that time."

"I just never ever want to even think about—"

"Who is Mick Cracken?!" Sarah asked again. This time the officers looked over at her.

"You mean you're not afraid of him?" Officer Bosendorfer said.

"I don't even know who he is."

"Well, don't tell him that." Officer Erard shook his head. "He hates that more than anything."

"Mick Cracken," Officer Bosendorfer said with a shudder, "is the most rotten, black-hearted buccaneer this side of the Big Dipper."

"He's dangerous," Officer Erard said.

"He's tough."

"He's strong."

"He's crazy."

"He once stole the hair off of the princess's cat."

"And the cat didn't even notice."

"He's dangerous."

"You already said that," Sarah said.

Officer Erard turned to Officer Bosendorfer. "You have to admit, he is clever though."

"Too clever."

"He's—"

A loud, piercing alarm sounded on the officers' uniforms. Officer Erard slumped farther down in his chair. "He's here."

"He's here?!" Sarah shrieked.

Officer Bosendorfer patted Sarah on the back. "We can only hope he doesn't steal you," he said gravely.

"Ha," Sarah said, "I'd love to see him try." But then she swallowed nervously.

Jacob Wonderbar jumped out of his chair and stood in front of the group. He didn't know what he planned to do, but he wasn't going to sit around and wait for this Mick Cracken to arrive and start stealing people. They had more important things to do, like figuring out if Earth still existed. The officers looked impressed by Jacob's sudden display of initiative and nodded to each other.

"We have to fight him," Jacob said.

Officer Erard threw his head back and laughed for

nearly thirty seconds. Then he seemed to realize that his laughter sounded a few shades away from outright lunacy and abruptly stopped. His face resumed its terrified countenance.

Officer Bosendorfer shuddered. "I only thought about his name that time," he said.

"If I may interrupt this *riveting* conversation that I was *so* looking forward to listening to for the next seven hours," the ship said, "my sensors are detecting an oncoming cruiser with a very snooty nav system bearing the royal insignia, who isn't shy about going on and on about his pedigree. Mick Cracken will be here in two minutes. Unless we do something now, we will be boarded and towed and I'll have to hear that nav system prattle on about his state-of-the-art rocket boosters for the next ten years, which may be the only thing in the universe that's less interesting than you hooligans."

Sarah sat forward. "Ship, what do you think we should do?"

"My name is Lucy," the ship snapped.

Sarah pursed her lips together. "What do you think we should do, *Lucy?*"

"Well," Lucy said with a suddenly unctuous and pleasing voice. "I just happened to be thinking that we could engage in some evasive maneuvers that I've been calculating, which I don't mind telling you are terribly exciting and employ geometric marvels beyond your pitiful human comprehension. We would do some rapid loops and twists while shooting off several spectacularly powerful missiles, and while you humans may be crippled by the resulting G forces and there is a seventeen percent chance that we would be blown to pieces by the missiles flying indiscriminately, I for one feel that it is well worth the trade-off. What do you say?"

Jacob and Sarah frowned at each other.

"That is," Lucy said, "unless you children are too frightened."

"I'm not scared of anything," Sarah said.

"I am," Dexter said. "I'm scared of many, many things."

Jacob looked out the cockpit window. He saw a little dark gray speck out in space. That little dark gray speck turned into a slightly larger little dark gray speck, and then it grew to such a size that it was no longer a speck at all but rather a dark gray splotch. The splotch grew larger and larger until Jacob could make out the contours of what could no longer be considered a speck nor a splotch but instead was definitely, positively a very large, very scary-looking spaceship that was rapidly heading their way.

"There he is!" Jacob shouted. "Evasive maneuvers!

We have to get away! But Lucy, no crippling maneuvers, and no missiles. That's an order."

"Fine," Lucy sighed. "But you should know that I'm already bored."

Lucy lurched into action and quickly left the police cruiser in the space dust. The kids and Officer Bosendorfer strapped themselves into their seats, while Officer Erard, who didn't have a seat, held on to the banister as best he could as Lucy turned at all-but-crippling speeds.

"This would be fun if we were on Planet Coasterland," Officer Erard said. "But we're not."

Jacob held on to his seat. The ship barreled into a long, arcing turn as Mick Cracken's vessel sped forward in an attempt to head them off. A deep mechanical voice filled the cabin. "Stop at once! You are about to have the immense honor of being boarded and relieved of your valuables by Mick Cracken, buccaneer, bandit, and brigand extraordinaire. Stop now or suffer extreme consequences."

"It's him," Officer Bosendorfer said. "Oh my, it's really him."

Mick Cracken was gaining on them, and no matter how snooty and royal Mick's ship may have been, it certainly had some advanced acceleration and steering capabilities that were preventing Lucy from escaping.

Mick's ship drew closer and closer. Jacob knew he had to do something.

"Lucy!" Jacob yelled. "Slam on the brakes. Slam on the brakes!"

Everyone was thrown forward in their seats as the spaceship abruptly stopped and Mick Cracken's ship sailed past. It receded into the distance, completely thrown off course.

"Wow, that actually worked! I can't believe it!" Jacob said.

Jacob turned back to slap Dexter high five. He was extremely thankful that they had watched *Top Gun* a couple of months earlier. He hadn't known at the time he was learning essential flying strategy.

"Talk to me, Maverick," Dexter said. "Bogey at twelve o'clock."

Jacob turned back in time to see Mick Cracken's ship execute an impossibly smooth, impossibly fast 180-degree turn. It came to a stop and paused for a moment, as if basking in the impressiveness of its execution, and then *wham*, it accelerated straight toward them. Danger was heading their way yet again, and danger happened to be driving a spaceship with state-of-the-art engines.

"Jake!" Sarah shrieked.

"Go! Go!" Jacob yelled. "Straight toward him. Try to sail right over."

Lucy accelerated and headed right toward Mick Cracken, who was just under ten seconds away in a collision course. Jacob knew it was their last chance to escape, assuming they were not all blown to smithereens in a head-on crash. Dexter covered his eyes. Sarah grabbed the edge of their seat. Officer Erard gripped the banister. Officer Bosendorfer shuddered. Mick's ship grew larger and larger in the cockpit window.

At the last possible moment Lucy tipped up and sailed right over Mick Cracken. Jacob looked back and sure enough, Mick Cracken's ship was headed the wrong way.

"We did it! We did it!" Jacob said. "Full speed ahead!"

Everyone lurched forward as Lucy instead came to an abrupt stop.

Dexter looked up at the window, which was now covered in thick mesh. "Is that rope?"

Jacob looked back and saw that Cracken had caught them in a massive net. "Oh no! Can we get out of this?"

Everything was still for a long, tense moment. Then they felt another lurch, and they slowly began moving in the direction of Mick Cracken's ship.

"We're being reeled in!" Sarah shouted.

Officer Bosendorfer solemnly patted Dexter and Sarah on their backs. "It was nice knowing you children."

CHAPTER 11

Dexter Goldstein stared up at the web of black cable that encircled the cockpit. Lucy had been pulled adjacent to Mick Cracken's ship, and they were all anxiously waiting to see what horrible fate he would bestow upon them. The cable looked rough and industrial and not at all futuristic, but had proven quite effective in keeping them from escaping.

"Don't you guys have tractor beams?" Dexter asked Officer Erard.

"Tractor who?"

Jacob returned from the storage room carrying an armful of blasters, launchers, and what appeared to be body armor. He tossed a blaster to Dexter, who looked at it for a moment before he set it down gently on the floor.

"Nuh-uh," Dexter said. "No way."

"Jake," Sarah said, "don't you think we should explore some nonviolent alternatives?"

"Like what?" Jake asked. "Who knows what this Mick Cracken person is going to do? I'm not going to let us get kidnapped or stolen or tortured. Not without a fight anyway."

"He'll definitely steal us." Officer Bosendorfer nodded. "I would try to arrest him, but he would probably steal my handcuffs."

There was a bang down below in the hold, and they heard the cargo door open and then close. Footsteps echoed across the wood plank floors. The footsteps reached the stairs, at which point the sound of the footsteps moved from the wood plank floors to the metal staircase. The footsteps slowly moved up the metal staircase until everyone in the cockpit saw a black helmet with a reflecting black visor. As the footsteps moved still closer, they saw that the helmet belonged to a small person wearing a black spacesuit, who walked up the remaining steps into the cockpit.

The small person took off his helmet, and a boy their age, with a mess of black hair, blue eyes, and a pale white face stood before them.

"Who are you?" Sarah asked, peering behind him to see if Mick Cracken was on his way up the stairs.

"Who am *I*?" the boy asked incredulously. Then he threw back his head and laughed loudly. "Oh. You're joking. That was good, you almost fooled me."

Jacob stepped over beside Sarah and cleared his throat. While he didn't point the blaster he was carrying at anyone in particular, he made sure it had a conspicuous presence in the proceedings. "No really, who are you? Where's Mick Cracken?"

Officers Erard and Bosendorfer stepped behind the boy and gestured frantically at Jacob, shaking their heads and mouthing, "No! No!" The boy saw Jacob looking over his shoulder, and he turned around to look at the officers, who abruptly stopped their wild gestures and instead raised their hands in surrender.

"Mr. Cracken," Officer Erard said. "Er, shall I say Mr. Cracken sir, uh, esquire . . . your most excellent excellency . . . uh . . . majesty. Officers Erard and Bosendorfer at your service."

Sarah Daisy's mouth dropped open. She looked at the kid again. He was barely taller than her. "*This* is Mick Cracken?"

Officer Erard winced. "She didn't mean that."

"*This* is the most fearsome buccaneer in the galaxy?" she asked.

Mick Cracken turned and winked at her. "Ah," he said with evident satisfaction. "So you do know who

I am. I thought so. I'm kind of famous, you know. Correction. Not 'kind of' famous. Extremely famous. Comes with the territory when you're as good of a thief as I am."

Jacob raised the blaster, and while he stopped short of pointing it directly at Mick, he did point it straight at the cockpit window in what he hoped was a some-what menacing gesture. "I'm going to have to ask you to step off of this ship," Jacob said.

"Young man," Officer Bosendorfer said. "I would advise against that."

Mick Cracken stepped toward Jacob. "And why should I be scared of that?" he asked, pointing at the blaster. "What are you going to do?"

Jacob knew that when dealing with bullies, the best opening strategy was a show of confidence to try to intimidate them, even if he didn't really want to fight. Jacob swallowed, mentally crossed his fingers that the cockpit shield was resistant to blasters, and pulled the trigger to fire a warning shot. He heard a pop, and a stream of brightly colored pink and yellow confetti rained down on everyone in the cockpit. "Happeeeee New Year!" the blaster shouted with a tinny voice, followed by sounds of cheering and glasses clinking.

Officer Bosendorfer glared at Jacob and brushed the confetti off of his uniform. "Young man, this is no time for a party."

Mick Cracken smirked and beckoned the group to follow him. "You're coming with me."

Officer Erard's shoulders slumped. He grabbed his helmet and started walking after Mick.

"Why should we go with you?" Dexter asked, and then covered his mouth as if he immediately regretted saying anything.

Mick stepped over and attempted to look Dexter in the eye, but Dexter avoided eye contact and instead pretended there was something across the cockpit that demanded his attention. "Because if you don't come with me, I'll blow this ship into a million pieces."

"That sounds reasonable," Dexter said quickly.

Jacob stepped between Dexter and Mick and tipped up his chin. "Leave him alone. Step back." Mick stood his ground and Jacob clenched his fists as he considered teaching Mick Cracken an interplanetary lesson. Mick grinned like he was ready for a fight.

But then Sarah Daisy stepped over and put her hand on Jacob's shoulder, and he unclenched his hands. He knew what she meant with the gesture, and he knew she was right, although he never would have admitted that to her out loud. Mick had Lucy trapped and they had no way of knowing how to get home. Jacob would have to find a way to escape that didn't involve pulverizing the ego out of any famous, or, correction, "extremely famous" bandits.

Jacob nodded to Dexter and Sarah. "Let's go see what his ship looks like." He tried to ignore Mick's triumphant smirk.

"Children," Lucy said with a pained sigh. "Please return to me as soon as possible so we can get out of this mess. I don't particularly like you very much, but I sure as Jupiter like you better than Mick Cracken's insufferable nav system."

"We will," Sarah said. "Thanks, Lucy."

Jacob, Dexter, and Sarah grabbed their space helmets and trudged down the stairs, following Mick Cracken and the space officers.

When they reached the cargo door, Jacob looked out into space at Mick Cracken's ship. Up close, Jacob saw that it wasn't actually dark gray, as he had originally thought, but rather a clumsily painted black. It was a rounded square and looked very ornate under the slapdash paint job, with majestic horses carved into the edges. There were dainty, almost feminine touches with swooping lacy swirls and flowers, and a hint of glittery silver peeked through some of the places where the black paint had worn off, almost as if . . .

"Is this a girl's ship?" Jacob asked.

Sarah Daisy looked over at Mick Cracken's ship and immediately saw what Jacob saw, namely that underneath the shoddy black paint was a spaceship that Cinderella wouldn't have minded taking to an outer space ball. She pointed and burst out laughing.

"Hey Mick," Jacob said with a big grin. "Maybe after we're done robbing aliens we can go take some space ponies for a picnic."

Mick glared at Jacob. "If you're asking if this ship once belonged to a girl, then yes, I personally stole it from the princess while evading the entire royal guard and half of the armed fleet. It is extremely fast, it is powerful, and as you can see from how easily I captured your own pitiful excuse for a ship, I have made some rather tremendous additions. Happy?"

Jacob nodded. "Yes. Yes, I am."

"It's a beautiful ship," Officer Erard said. "I wish I had such a wonderful ship. Truly a specimen."

"One in a million," Officer Bosendorfer said. "My eyes hurt from looking at its spectacular . . . ocity, uh, ness. I would arrest you for stealing it from the princess were it not for the fact that your father would surely—"

"Don't talk about my father!" Mick Cracken turned around and jabbed them both in the chest with his finger. "That's it, you're walking the star plank!"

Officer Bosendorfer exhaled and nodded, his face relaxing. "Thank you Mr. Cracken," he whispered with a quiet shudder. "Thank you for showing us mercy."

"Helmets on, everyone," Mick said. "Let's go."

Jacob, Sarah, and Dexter put on their helmets and followed Mick and the space officers as they stepped out into the vacuum and sailed through space toward Mick Cracken's ship. Jacob allowed himself a quick glance back at Lucy, all wrapped up in knotted cable. Even though Lucy was the ship that had taken them so many billions of miles from home, away from their families and from Earth, somehow the fifty yards between her and Mick's ship seemed even greater than all those miles they'd traveled. Home was now a lot farther than just a comfortable spaceship ride away.

He had no idea how he would get back to Lucy, let alone back through the Spilled Milky Way galaxy and through the solar system and back to his house on the little block where all the houses looked the same. If home was still there at all.

Mick escorted the officers to the top of the ship, and Jacob followed them. He stood atop the ship in the blackness of space and stared at Mick's shiny helmet, wondering what he would do.

After a long, deliberate pause, during which Jacob imagined Mick silently gloating that he had their undivided attention, Mick reached down and pressed a button. A thin plank extended out from the ship into space.

"Walk the star plank!" Mick yelled through the intercom, using his vocal modifier to lower his voice. He jabbed the officers in the back.

"Good-bye, children," Officer Bosendorfer said.

"Now!" Mick shouted.

Officers Bosendorfer and Erard shuffled to the edge of the plank and stared out into space. They turned back to give the group one wave good-bye and then they stepped off the plank one after the other.

Jacob, Sarah, and Dexter rushed over to the edge and saw Officers Bosendorfer and Erard sailing comfortably and safely through space. They turned back to

wave once more before they continued on in the direction of their police cruiser.

Mick joined Jacob, Sarah, and Dexter at the edge of the ship, watching the officers spacewalk away. "I wish there were water and sharks and alligators. It would be so much more fun." He sighed. "Oh well." He turned to Jacob, Sarah, and Dexter. "Who wants to go steal something?"

CHAPTER 12

Dexter walked around Mick's spaceship and marveled at the massive ordeal the ship had clearly undergone after Mick had stolen it. Pre-Mick the ship had evidently been a princess's luxury cruiser, with rooms of pink and purple, massive walk-in closets, statues of horses and lap dogs, stuffed animals, and plush carpet galore. Post-Mick the walls were covered with garish graffiti, ornate fixtures had been broken and strewn about, and the ship looked as if it had not been cleaned in several months. Dexter stared in particular at a large, beautifully painted portrait of a brunette girl, upon which Mick had drawn horns, thick eyebrows, and a large curling mustache.

"Um. Don't take this the wrong way, but do you have psychological problems?" Dexter asked.

Mick stood beside Dexter and looked at the defaced painting. "Trust me, it's an improvement."

Sarah Daisy walked around the ship munching on a cucumber sandwich and sipping a glass of tea in a dainty porcelain cup. The tea had been highly recommended by Praiseworthy, the ship's nav system, whose voice followed her around the ship no matter which room she was in. Sarah *uh-huh*ed occasionally out of politeness, but Praiseworthy did not need any encouragement to continue speaking.

"Oh, we've had the most wonderful and dangerous adventures," Praiseworthy said in his exceedingly proper accent. "I am operating fully outside of my capacities, but the excitement, the dramatics, the theatrics! My previous owner was Mistress Silver Spoon, which is Master Cracken's name for Her Highness, not mine, and you shan't tell Master Cracken I said this, but she is *quite* a lovely young lady, but you see I just always wanted to be a pirate ship, or dare I say a buccaneer ship because Master Cracken feels that buccaneer is a more impressive name than pirate, which is just so pedestrian, don't you think? Have I told you about my rocket boosters? No? They are quite advanced and—"

"So listen up." Mick waited for a few long seconds to build anticipation, and gathered Jacob, Sarah, and Dexter around. "We're going to steal . . ."

After waiting a few moments for Mick to finish, Dexter said, "We're going to steal what?"

Mick paused a few more seconds for good measure. "We're going to steal . . . the Dragon's Eye."

Mick waited expectantly for a reaction. Jacob, Dexter, and Sarah looked at one another, and since none of them showed any hint of recognition, they unanimously reached the conclusion that they had never heard of a Dragon's Eye.

"We're not impressed," Sarah said. "Look, Cracken, we really need to see if our planet is okay."

Mick rolled his eyes. "Earth? Who cares. I'm sure it's fine."

"How do you know?" Jacob asked.

"People. Dragon's Eye. The biggest diamond in the galaxy. Focus." Mick waited for them to react with suitable excitement, but when it was clear they didn't know what he was talking about, he continued: "A long time ago some space explorers came across an asteroid orbiting a planet in a backwater corner of the galaxy. The planet was tiny, dusty, and not very interesting, and it smelled like burp breath. So everyone left it alone. But then some explorers were in trouble because their ship was having mechanical problems, so they decided to land on the planet, even though it smelled like burp breath."

"Quite right," Praiseworthy said. "Fine storytelling, Master Cracken, and if I may interject . . ."

"As the explorers were trying to land, they crashed into a foreign object. It was about twenty feet in diameter, and it seriously damaged their ship. It was the asteroid. But here's the thing. When the ship issued a distress call, they swore that they had been hit by a huge, pure, perfectly round diamond. A diamond twenty feet in diameter. The single biggest diamond in the galaxy."

Sarah looked at Jacob and Dexter and shrugged. "Still not impressed."

"What happened to the explorers?" Dexter asked.

"Who cares, they probably landed on the planet and smelled bad. The point is, the biggest diamond had been discovered, and the people who received the distress call went and found it. They could have sold it and gotten rich beyond their wildest dreams, but instead they completely lost their minds and donated it to science." Mick leaned in. "What do you say we do the right thing and steal it? I just need a few subordinates for my plan to work."

"We really should be trying to get back home," Sarah said.

"Agreed," Dexter said.

Mick sneered and shook his head. "You have to be

joking. It's a huge diamond!" When none of the children signaled that they were changing their minds, Mick waved for them to lean in closer. He looked around carefully, as if someone could possibly be eavesdropping on them on a ship in the middle of nowhere in outer space. "What if I told you this diamond has the power to grant a wish?"

"What kind of a wish?" Sarah asked.

"Any wish," Mick said. "The Dragon's Eye is more than just a diamond. It's a machine. The greatest machine ever created. It uses quantum manipulation to create any possibility in the entire universe. It can create anything out of thin air. All you have to do is place your hand on the Dragon's Eye and wish."

"How many wishes?" Dexter asked. "Can you wish for a million wishes?"

Mick smiled. "There's only one way to find out. Why do you think I want to steal it so badly?"

Jacob narrowed his eyes. He didn't think there was any possible way a diamond could grant a wish, no matter how much technology they had in outer space. And as a highly skilled liar himself, he was fairly good at knowing when someone wasn't telling the truth. "I don't believe you," he said. He turned to Sarah and Dexter. "He's full of it. Let's get out of here."

"Jake," Sarah whispered, "if you told me yesterday

that it was possible to fly through the solar system in a talking spaceship I would have thought you were bonkers. What if the wish thing is true? We could wish ourselves back to Earth! If it was destroyed maybe we could wish it back to life! How else are we going to get back home?"

"I agree," Dexter whispered. "The quantum whatever thing seems possible."

"He's lying," Jacob said through clenched teeth.

Sarah shook her head and turned away from Jacob. "I want to go for it," she said to Mick.

"I'll go if she goes," Dexter said.

Mick Cracken looked at Jacob and beamed. "Well, well, well. Seems as if your friends are the smart ones. You shouldn't be surprised. I'm very persuasive."

"Oh, jolly day," Praiseworthy said. "How I love adventure. Master Cracken, I do wish you would find me a proper buccaneer flag to display. My fellow cruise liners would be so jealous if they knew what dangerous voyages I was embarking upon."

Jacob couldn't believe that his friends sided with Mick and his stupid diamond instead of him. They didn't even care what he thought. He was billions of miles away from home. Billions. They had been gone for hours. But even those hours and billions of miles weren't as long and vast as the twelve years of friendship that had just been fractured by the appearance of Mick Cracken.

Jacob turned and walked away.

"Jake," Sarah said.

But Jacob didn't stop. He could feel Mick's smile burning a hole in his back.

CHAPTER 13

Jacob sat in the rear hold of Mick Cracken's ship, and as he often did when he was upset, he thought about his father. Jacob's dad was the type of person who was a little too much fun for his own good. He would always dress up like Sherlock Holmes with a crazy hat and wooden pipe on Jacob's birthday and give Jacob clues about where he could find his presents, although sometimes he would end up forgetting where he hid them. Everyone liked him because of his silliness, and Jacob grew used to hearing his friends and classmates say his dad was cool. Jacob really wanted to believe them, even though his dad had a special talent for turning ordinary events into catastrophes. When he took Jacob fishing in the mountains one time he ignited a massive lighter-fluid soaked campfire that quickly spread to a nearby bush, and Jacob had to help stamp out the flames. Only Jacob Wonderbar and a North Face sleeping bag stood between a fatherly mishap and a raging forest fire, but thankfully boy and camping gear were up to the task. They never caught any fish either.

Sometimes Jacob's dad would look at him like he was surprised that Jacob was there. It was as if he couldn't imagine that life had given him a small person who followed him around and depended upon him and had the same color eyes but different color skin and represented the one thing in his life that perhaps needed to be taken somewhat seriously. So while Jacob was too old and had seen too many movies to think that his parents' divorce was his fault exactly, he knew that he was a part of it. Not that he drove his parents apart because he was so much trouble to deal with, but rather he knew that his dad couldn't really picture himself being a dad. Jacob was a human-sized shirt that didn't fit. His dad looked at Jacob and saw a kid, and the presence of that kid made him an adult, and adults were people who grew old and died. Jacob's dad left his kid and ran away so he could go be a kid himself again. But knowing that didn't make it any easier.

Jacob didn't want to be like his dad, and yet he knew he had gotten himself into a mess that would make his dad's antics look tiny and inconsequential in comparison.

Jacob heard footsteps, and Sarah Daisy came around the corner. She tipped up her head a little in greeting and sat down beside him without saying a word.

They sat together a while, staring at the pink walls of the spaceship's hold, and Jacob thought about how long he had known Sarah Daisy. He remembered the time she hit him with a well-aimed rock when she was in second grade and the time she came over to his house, rang the doorbell, and quietly gave him a flattened four-leaf clover when she found out his dad had left.

"I know you're mad," she said.

"I'm not mad."

Sarah turned her head a little and looked at Jacob out of the corner of her eye.

"I'm not," he said.

"Jake . . ."

"I'm happy for you guys. Go get your diamond. Whatever. I'll find my own way back."

"Be serious," she said.

"I am being serious. If you want to follow a demented kid pirate around the galaxy, go right ahead."

"He's not a demented pirate."

"Oh, excuse me, a demented *buccaneer*. And you

clearly have Dexter wrapped around your finger, so you can both go and run off together."

Sarah didn't say anything. She rubbed her nose and cleared her throat. "So just now, were you thinking about your dad?" she asked.

Jacob didn't say anything.

"I know you probably miss him a lot even though he's a total jerk for leaving you behind."

Jacob stared at the floor. "Don't call him that."

"Sorry," she said. "But anyway, this diamond thing isn't about our friendship or whatever. I really don't know what to do. How else are we going to get home to see if everything's okay?"

Jacob just nodded, even though he didn't believe the diamond even existed. He had to admit that he didn't really know what to do either. They were quiet for a little while, and then Jacob pulled out a crumpled photograph and handed it to Sarah.

It was a picture of Mick Cracken in knee-high socks, black shorts, suspenders, and a top hat, and he looked like he was in the middle of a dance. The expression on his face was so sour he was clearly aware that he was wearing an outfit that probably would have gotten him kicked out of the Outer Space Buccaneer Guild.

"I found it in one of the storerooms."

Sarah let out a high-pitched giggle, and then raised her hand to her mouth, wondering where such a laugh came from. Jacob flinched because usually when Sarah was embarrassed she found a way to inflict physical pain on him, so Jacob was surprised when she instead she just bumped him gently, shoulder to shoulder.

"You're a good guy, Jake," she said.

CHAPTER 14

Dexter Goldstein watched Mick draw a big spiral on the wall with a large black marker as a mechanical duck followed Mick around the room. Dexter was unimpressed by the creativity or talent reflected in the sloppy drawing, but he had to admit it lent a certain sense of earnest destruction to Mick's massive opus of graffiti art.

"So, uh, are you really from outer space?" Dexter asked.

Mick stopped drawing on the wall long enough to smirk at Dexter. "You really don't know where Astrals came from?"

Dexter didn't have time to answer because Sarah and Dexter returned to the cabin. Mick tried to pretend that he was still interested in his graffiti art, though Dexter could tell he was waiting to see what Jacob was going to say.

"All right, Mick," Jacob said. "We're in. Let's go find this diamond."

"Great goose's gold!" Praiseworthy said. "Master Wonderbar, I could not be more excited that you have chosen to embark on this voyage, I dare say a good gentlemanly camaraderie makes every adventure—"

"Ahem," Sarah said. "Gentlemanly?"

"Oh dear me, Mistress Daisy, I didn't mean to exclude you, all I meant to say was that—"

"You don't think girls make good thieves?"

"The best thieves, Mistress Daisy, the best thieves," Praiseworthy said quickly. "It's just that—"

"Well, well, well," Mick interrupted, putting a finishing flourish on a stick figure making a rude gesture. "So the Dragon's Eye slays another. I knew you would come around."

"Where is it?" Jacob asked.

"Oh, don't worry. I know where it is. I would just like to savor this moment." Mick took a deep breath and smiled with his eyes closed. "Ahh. There. It's so fun hatching a plan. Especially when even your rival sees the genius in it."

"It doesn't take a genius to chase after a diamond," Jacob said.

"No? Maybe you would like to lead us to the diamond that you had never heard of until five minutes ago, and that you still at this moment have no idea where to find?"

Mick let the long pause stretch on.

"I thought not. Looks like I'm the leader. Reluctantly. It's not easy being the one with a vision, but it's a burden I choose to accept. After all, who was the one who stole seven out of the eight moons from Orion's belt?"

Dexter shrugged his shoulders.

"It was me," Mick said.

Jacob couldn't wait to shut Mick up. "I really didn't want to have to do this." He walked over to Dexter and showed him the photograph of Mick dressed up in his top hat.

Dexter spasmed with sharp laughter. He pointed at the picture in disbelief. "Oh man. You are so busted."

Mick's face turned red and he started to walk toward Dexter, but Praiseworthy chimed in, "Master Cracken, I have some urgent news. The royal fleet is approaching, and there are a great many of them. I fear they are trying to encircle us."

Mick ran out of the room. "Let's go!" he shouted.

Jacob, Sarah, and Dexter followed him into the cockpit, which was filled with video screens that provided a view in every direction of space. The ship's instruments were plated in gold, something even Mick didn't seem to have the heart to deface. Mick typed furiously into the interface and stared at the monitors, which were filled with ominous X's.

"They're everywhere. This is not good."

Jacob looked out into space and saw red ships spaced at regular intervals, all of them bearing down quickly.

"Praiseworthy, evasive action Beta. Step on it!" Mick shouted.

Praiseworthy yelled a still-proper-sounding "Yee-haw!" and space seemed to blur a little as they accelerated. The ships quickly grew in size as they drew near but then flew harmlessly by as Praiseworthy easily left them behind, even though he still had the extra burden of towing Lucy.

"Wow," Sarah said. "Praiseworthy, I didn't know you had it in you."

"Oh Mistress Daisy, how it pleases me to hear you say that. Did I mention my rocket boosters? There really is nothing like them in the universe, and Master Cracken—"

"What can we do to help?" Jacob asked.

Mick pounded a few more instruments and kept his eye on the monitors. "Now that you mention it, you and Dexter could go into the rear gunner room. It has a red door. Go in there and fire some warning shots to keep them off our tail."

Jacob nodded and they ran into the rear of the ship. They found the red door, which opened with a hiss. Jacob and Dexter stepped inside the small room, which had a small porthole for a window. The door closed with another hiss and they held on as the ship began to shake violently.

Dexter looked around. "The gun has to be here somewhere."

Jacob grabbed Dexter and placed a finger to his lips. "Praiseworthy?" he said. "Can you hear me?"

Praiseworthy didn't say anything, and Jacob thought that he might be too busy escaping the fleet.

"I'd really like to hear more about your rocket boosters."

Praiseworthy still didn't say anything. He was safely occupied. Jacob didn't have much time if he wanted to accomplish the plan he had just concocted.

"Dexter, listen. If Mick Cracken is the scariest buccaneer in the galaxy, who do you think those ships are?"

Dexter frowned. "Uh, the royal fleet?"

"Exactly. If Mick's the bad guy, they're the good guys! They might be able to get us out of this!"

Dexter paused to think about it. "I don't know about that. Mick may be a buccaneer and all, and between you and me I think he might have some mental issues, but he doesn't seem like that bad of a guy."

"I don't trust him! You and I can take Mick. We can take control of this situation. Let's steal Mick's spaceship, turn him in, and go figure out what happened to Earth!"

Jacob was waiting for a rousing agreement, but instead Dexter was staring out the window into space.

"Dexter?"

Dexter leaned back and pointed at the window, his face suddenly pale.

Jacob looked out into space and saw Mick's ship and Lucy, still tied up with rope, receding into the distance.

"Is that . . . Praiseworthy? Why would we be moving away from Praiseworthy? What's happening?"

In a flash, Jacob realized they weren't in a gunner room at all. They were slowly drifting through outer space, away from Praiseworthy and Mick and Lucy and Sarah and any hope they had of finding their way back home to Earth.

They were in an emergency pod. Mick had fired them off into the great unknown.

"I think we've been jettisoned," Dexter said.

CHAPTER 15

You did what?!" Sarah shouted.

"I knew you'd be pleased," Mick said, relaxing back into his captain's chair with a wide grin.

"Pleased?! Why would I be pleased?"

Mick frowned and held up a finger to signal for time. After a moment he said, "Wait. Let me get this straight. You actually like those people?"

"Yes, you imbecile!"

Mick scratched his chin as if he were trying to solve a complex mathematical problem. "Huh. I hardly even remember their names. Are they important people on your planet? I don't trust the guy named Wondersomething, he didn't like the plan. You can't steal something with people you don't trust. That's practically rule number one of being a buccaneer."

Sarah felt her face flush and she suddenly wished that her mom had let her take martial arts instead of ballet, because she would have loved to use Mick Cracken's thick head as target practice. She balled her hands into fists and hit her chair, pounding the soft cushion again and again until her knuckles stung. She heard her mom's voice in her head lecturing her that proper ladies don't throw temper tantrums, and she hit the cushion one more time for good measure.

"I am not a lady!" Sarah yelled at Mick.

Mick had a scared smile locked on his face.

"I can't believe this!" Sarah said. "I can't believe you left my friends behind. Turn this ship around, Praiseworthy. We're going back to get them."

Mick swallowed, and he tapped his cheek with his finger. "Um. Well. We can't. We left the royal fleet behind, but if we turned back we'd definitely be captured."

"*You'd* be captured," Sarah said. "I haven't done anything wrong. Praiseworthy!"

"Well, you see Mistress Daisy, I must be commanded by Master Cracken, and since he doesn't wish to go back, I shan't disobey his orders, but all the same I do wish you would reconsider, as I was so looking forward to embarking upon adventures with you. And if I may be perfectly honest, I am not ready to return to life as a pleasure cruiser. There is always a great deal of shrieking and talking about boys. It's simply dreadful."

Mick cleared his throat. "It's just you and me, Sarah. Well. And Praiseworthy."

Sarah gave Mick a fierce gaze that she hoped would burn his eyebrows off.

Mick put on what Sarah assumed was his best roguish grin, which simply irritated her further. "I thought you wanted to go find the Dragon's Eye with me," he said.

Sarah jumped up and stared Mick Cracken right in the face. "You thought wrong."

Sarah stomped out of the cockpit and marched around the ship until she found a stateroom with a large four-post bed. She jumped up onto the bed, grabbed a headless stuffed animal, and threw it against the wall, where it collided with a soft thud.

"Ouch!" Praiseworthy said.

"Sorry, Praiseworthy."

"Actually, I can't feel pain. That was a joke. Was it funny? Oh, how I hope it was funny. I just can't bear to think that you're unhappy."

Sarah sighed and tried to still be mad, although a bit less successfully than before. She imagined Jake and Dexter, trapped in some small escape pod, pressing buttons and arguing with each other, and the thought of her two best friends fighting it out made her a bit less angry as well. If she knew Jacob Wonderbar, he'd have a plan in no time, and not even a trip into the middle of Nowheresville, Outer Space, would scare him. Then she had an image of Jake finding his way back and freeing her from Mick's ship and giving Mick a good punch in the nose and saving the day . . .

Sarah sat straight up in bed. She was actually daydreaming about a *boy* saving *her*? Sarah shook her head violently. What in the world was happening to her? Her hero Betty Friedan would be so ashamed. Sarah looked up at the ceiling.

"Sorry, Betty. I promise that I do not need a boy to save me, nor do I want such a thing to happen, because women are perfectly able to save themselves, and they most certainly do not need a boy to help them."

Sarah remembered all the times boys had slighted her in the past few hours. Jacob hadn't even let her look for the spaceship and then he took the captain's seat himself and created a horrible space mess, and worst of all, the miscreant Mick Cracken had taken it upon himself to ditch her friends without even considering that she might be upset about it. She clutched her hands into fists at the mere thought of that pretend pirate, who had actually believed she would be impressed by his silly antics and who had the nerve to fire her friends into space. He had actually thought she would like to be stuck on a spaceship with him, so typical of boys, who are all so conceited they can hardly see anything beyond their pointy noses. Soon enough she was punching her pillow and had roused herself into a spirited sense of indignation.

"That's it!" she shouted to no one in particular. She jumped out of bed, stomped through the room, and flung open the door, which smacked right into the face of Mick Cracken.

"Ow," he said, rubbing his forehead.

"You were spying on me?"

"No! Well, yes."

"Ugh!" Sarah marched toward the rear of the ship and Mick tried to keep up.

"What are you doing?"

Sarah knew perfectly well what she was doing. She was going to put on her space helmet, cut Lucy loose, and fly back to find Jacob Wonderbar and Dexter Goldstein. She wasn't going to wait for a boy to save her. She would set things right and get them all back home safely to Earth, or at least . . . Her breath caught when she thought of her sister, The Brat, and her parents and her piano and her cat, Susan B. Anthony, and she hoped they were all safe. She needed to get back and she wouldn't let a stupid space pirate stop her.

"You're not trying to escape, are you?"

Sarah turned around and pushed on Mick's forehead with her finger.

"Bingo."

She whirled back around and kept walking until she reached the rear door of the ship. All she needed was her helmet and she would be ready to leave.

"Cracken!" she shouted. "Where's my—"

When she looked behind her she saw Mick holding her helmet. He offered it to her.

"Here," he said.

Sarah played it very cool as she tried to make sense of Mick's sudden helpfulness. She eyed him suspiciously and snatched back her helmet even though Mick didn't try to keep it from her. All she had to do was open the cargo door and she would be on her way back to Jacob and Dexter.

"You're not going to try and stop me?" she asked.

Mick stared down at his space boots. "I don't want to keep anyone here against their will. Especially not a friend."

"I'm not your friend," Sarah said, although she hesitated in front of the cargo door. She stared at the large red button and wondered if there was a force field around it that was preventing her from doing the sensible thing and pushing it. It was as if the Dragon's Eye was using its magical powers to hold her back.

Mick still had a mournful expression on his face, but Sarah thought she saw a new glint in his eye. "You know, the Dragon's Eye is still out there, just waiting to be stolen . . ."

Sarah's hand hovered over the red button even longer. It seemed like he was reading her mind. Even if she did escape with Lucy, she had no way of knowing how to get around the space kapow. The Dragon's Eye might be her ticket home. She imagined herself placing her hands on the diamond and wishing them all back to Earth, and if they found out Earth was gone she could use the Dragon's Eye to save the entire world. She knew full well what a strong and determined girl could accomplish on her own. All she needed was the opportunity to show them all.

"And why should I believe you'll help me?" Sarah asked.

"You think I'd risk breaking a promise I made to you?"

"You'd better not."

"I wouldn't."

"Because I would break you into a

million pieces and they'd never even find the pieces because I'd scatter them around the galaxy in a thousand
different places so you could never, ever be put back
together."

Mick cleared his throat. "Buccaneer's honor."

She had to try to save her family back on Earth.
Jacob and Dexter had each other. They would be
fine.

Sarah slammed her hand on the big red button on
the cargo door control panel and looked out the win-

dow. The ropes that were holding Lucy slipped away. She was free.

Sarah wouldn't be joining her. She had a big wish-granting diamond to steal. She would show Jacob and Dexter who should be in charge.

"Let's go get it," Sarah said.

CHAPTER 16

"Mayday! Mayday!" Dexter shouted. "Maaay-daaay!!"

"No one can hear us. You don't have to yell."

"They invented that word for a reason! It means, 'Please please please for the love of God someone rescue me!' Maaydaay!!"

Jacob and Dexter had been floating aimlessly in space for just a few moments when the pod's rocket boosters flared and began propelling them at a rapid speed through the galaxy. They had taken turns staring out the window at the stars and planets racing by, but the pod showed no signs of stopping.

The escape pod was only about eight feet in diameter, and was sparsely furnished, with only a few cabinets full of meager supplies, including water and some pastries, a couple of flashlights, a makeup kit, and a portable pink porcelain tea set. Jacob stared at the instrument panel, which didn't seem to have buttons or anything he could control. All he could see was their speed, trajectory, and the destination, which was listed as "Numonia."

"Have you heard of a planet called Numonia?"

Dexter's jaw quivered. "I knew it. We're definitely going to die."

"We're not going to die!"

"We're heading toward a planet named after an infectious disease! Of course we're going to die!"

"It's spelled differently! I'm pretty sure there's a *p* in *pneumonia*."

Dexter leaned against the wall of the pod. He stared at the ceiling and his foot began to fidget uncontrollably. "We need to think."

"Good idea. Let's think."

Jacob placed fingers to his temples. He had once read an article that said that the part of the brain responsible for inspiration activated when you stopped thinking of anything and let your brain relax. Jacob took a deep breath and quieted his mind. He felt the cool air-conditioning on his skin. He heard the whirring of the gears of the pod and the strange whoosh as it passed through the vacuum of space. He heard his heart beating in his ears. He heard Dexter hyperventilating.

What he didn't hear was his brain thinking of any good ideas.

"Mayday!!" Jacob yelled.

"Mayday!!" Dexter started laughing uncontrollably. "Mayday!!! Ha-ha-ha! Wow. Now I'm so scared I don't even care what happens anymore." He reached over and patted Jacob on the shoulder. "Thanks, Wonderbar. I needed a laugh."

"You're welcome."

Although he didn't know where in the universe they were headed, Jacob at least was able to comfort himself with the knowledge that Sarah surely had discovered what Mick had done to them. He smiled to think of the horrific tantrum Mick Cracken must have been witnessing at that very moment and how much Mick must be regretting discovering the explosive side of Sarah Daisy.

Jacob and Dexter were in a tough spot, but if he knew Sarah, nothing could stop her from turning Praiseworthy around and rescuing them the second she found out they were missing.

"Um. Wonderbar?" Dexter was staring out of the window and shaking his head. "I think you might want to take a look at this."

Jacob stepped over to the window, and suddenly red lights and a loud horn started blaring.

"Ah! Ah! I knew it was bad!" Dexter shouted.

Jacob watched a tiny gray planet growing larger and larger.

"Wonderbar!"

"I see it!"

The planet grew closer and closer as the pod rocketed toward it.

"We're going too fast!" Dexter yelled.

The planet couldn't have been more than a few miles across, but they were on a head-on course at an incredible speed. Jacob grasped the walls of the pod as tightly as he could.

"Hold on!" he yelled.

They were going way too fast toward a very ugly planet. The gray texture of the planet took shape. Jacob saw a glint of silver as the planet grew closer.

"We're going to crash!"

Jacob felt his stomach fling into his throat as the boosters fired.

The pod landed gently.

"Oh."

When the dust settled, Jacob looked out the window at an empty gray planet. The pod hatch opened.

Dexter sniffed the air. "Is that . . . burp breath?"

CHAPTER 17

Dexter and Jacob sat on the ground in front of the escape pod and looked at their surroundings. At first they had enjoyed jumping around on the surface of the planet, which, because of its small size, had much less gravity than Earth. Jacob jumped ten feet in the air and pretended to do a 360-degree somersault tomahawk jam into an imaginary hoop. Dexter countered with a between-the-legs behind-the-back eyes-covered Statue of Liberty, but soon they both began to cough on the planet's air, which still smelled like burp breath, so they sat down instead.

Dexter rubbed his skin. "Wow, I'm getting hot."

Just then the sun receded, a cool breeze blew, and they were plunged into darkness. The temperature plummeted.

Dexter kept rubbing his skin. "Um, now I'm cold."

Thirty seconds later the sun came up again.

"Hot," Dexter said.

Thirty seconds after that it was night again.

"Cold."

"This could take some getting used to," Jacob said.

When the sun rose again Jacob scanned the horizon. He could see nothing but grayness. The ground was covered in a squishy gray dust unlike anything he'd seen before. It stuck together very easily, almost like Silly Putty, but when pulled apart it crumbled back into dust. Jacob formed a handful of it into a small clump that resembled a warm gray snowball. He sniffed it and then handed it over to Dexter.

"I dare you to eat this."

"No way!"

"Just a bite. I'll give you my Ho Hos the next time we're at lunch."

Dexter looked at the dustball again, and Jacob could tell he was seriously considering the proposal. The Goldsteins were health nuts, and Dexter possessed a fiendish craving for sugar. But Jacob dropped the dustball and stood up.

"I see someone."

A small man had appeared on the horizon and he was slowly making his way toward the pod.

"Who is that?" Dexter yelled.

"Shhh!"

They felt a breeze and then they were plunged into darkness. Jacob could no longer see the man and he grabbed Dexter, knowing that the man could be racing toward them.

When the sun rose, the man was still standing where Jacob had last seen him. But he started walking toward them again. It took two days (or two minutes) for the man to reach the pod. He was wearing brown pants and a gray shirt that appeared to be made out of plastic. His skin was wrinkled and spotted, and his gray hair was combed over a mostly bald head. He stood in front of the pod, staring at Dexter and Jacob, before his face broke into a friendly smile.

"Moonman McGillicutty at your service! Welcome to Numonia. I think you're going to like it here. Where are you from?"

"Earth," Dexter said.

"Oh dear me, I'm sorry about that. Numonia is way better than Earth."

Jacob and Dexter looked at each other and out at the planet. Jacob couldn't see a television, basketball hoop, game system, or even a wisp of grass anywhere. In fact, he couldn't see anything but grayness. And then there was the matter of the air smelling like burp breath.

"We saw your pod landing on our fair planet, and me and the missus and some of the other esteemed residents of Numonia would like to invite you fellas to a . . ."

Jacob felt a breeze, and night fell. Numonia was covered in darkness. In the soft light emanating from the pod, Jacob could see that Moonman McGillicutty had fallen asleep standing on his feet. He began to snore loudly. Thirty seconds later the sun rose, and Moonman yawned and stretched.

"Good morning, pardners! Hope you got a good night's sleep."

Dexter said, "We didn't . . ."

"Anyway, as I was saying," Moonman said, "we would like to invite you fellas to a banquet. We don't have too many visitors, probably because folks know that when they visit Numonia they'll love it so much they just want to stay forever."

Dexter had one of his sudden coughing fits, and Jacob patted him on the back. Dexter stared at Jacob with his eyes wide open as he tried to regain his breath.

Jacob couldn't imagine how they could possibly get off Numonia. The pod was only designed for a one-way trip and probably didn't have any fuel left. No one besides Sarah and Mick Cracken knew where they were, and he was confident that Numonia didn't see too many visitors. Jacob remembered the glint of silver he saw when they were crashing down to the planet, and he wondered if it was a ship. Whatever Moonman McGillicutty's intentions, Jacob knew they only had one choice: Make friends with the locals and try to think of a plan.

"We'd love to," Jacob said.

Dexter started coughing again.

Moonman beamed. "Right this way! It's a ten-day walk, so I hope you boys are well rested."

Dexter and Jacob bounced after Moonman and tried to get used to walking with less gravity. They made their way over the horizon, stopping every thirty seconds so Moonman could get his nightly sleep, and soon spied a large, crashed silver spaceship along with some small huts made out of the Numonian dust.

"That's the spaceship Swift. Our wonderful ancestors were exploring this region of the galaxy when they hit a big diamond and crashed. Turned out they got something better than a diamond." Moonman beamed, putting his arms around Dexter's and Jacob's shoulders and giving them a collegial hug. "They got Numonia."

"Haven't you ever tried to leave?" Dexter asked.

Moonman stopped and sputtered, searching for words. "What . . . Why . . . Why would we want to do a thing like that? I . . . Have you noticed this weather? One hundred four thousand, seven hundred eighty-three days of sunshine a year!"

The boys heard a whoop, and a large woman with long blond hair came rushing over from one of the huts.

"That would be Stargirl McGillicutty," Moonman said with a wink. "My better half."

Just before Stargirl reached them, night fell and Moonman and Stargirl promptly went to sleep, snoring loudly in concert. Jacob and Dexter waited for them to wake up.

"Good morning, children!" Stargirl shouted when she awoke, pressing Dexter and Jacob to her large body in an enveloping hug. "Welcome to Numonia! Did you sleep well? Has Moonman told you about the Tree of Life? Did you, Moonman?"

"Didn't want to overwhelm the boys. There will be plenty of time to show them the wonders of Numonia. I suspect they'll be here awhile." He winked at the boys again.

"Oh, but you have to!" Stargirl turned to the boys. "It is the most incredible sight you will ever see in your lives. You must see it, you simply must."

"Whaddya say, boys? It's a five-week walk. You up for it?"

Jacob turned away and looked over at the spaceship Swift. It had a large dent in the front from the Dragon's Eye, but it looked like it might be space-worthy. Jacob wanted to rush over there and fly off the planet and go find Sarah, but when he looked back at Moonman McGillicutty he saw such hopefulness and eagerness in his face. Jacob knew he had to keep the locals happy if he was going to have a shot at stealing their ship.

"Actually," Dexter said. "What we really need is to—"

"Sure," Jacob said. "Let's go see the Tree of Life."

"Jacob . . ." Dexter whispered. "Maybe we should—"

"Dexter is even more excited to see it than I am." Jacob smirked at Dexter.

Dexter crossed his arms and narrowed his eyes at Jacob, but he didn't argue.

The McGillicuttys whooped with excitement, and the four of them began the less-than-arduous five-week walk to the Tree of Life. The rest of the planet looked identical to the stretches Jacob and Dexter had already seen. Gray, gray, and more gray. As they walked, Moonman told them about the North and South poles of Numonia, which they never visited because it never got completely dark there and they couldn't sleep. "We stay in the middle of the planet so we can get our rest,"

Stargirl said. Jacob kicked the dust and jumped a few times just for fun, but the trip was slow going with the McGillicuttys stopping to sleep (and snore) every time it was night.

Finally, after a little over a half hour of walking, they were on the other side of the planet. That's when Jacob saw the Tree of Life.

It was a stubby stick poking out of the ground. Its worn wood was wrinkled, knobby, and twisted, and it only rose about four feet into the air. Two small yellow leaves clung to the bark for dear life. Jacob was fearful of breathing too heavily lest the tree fall over and wither away completely.

Tears formed in Moonman's eyes and he solemnly grasped Jacob and Dexter with trembling hands.

"Isn't it magnificent?" he whispered.

CHAPTER 18

mick and Sarah peered around the corner at the front of the museum. It was a tall building shaped like a massive beaker, and the sunlight glinted off its bright surface. A large banner above the entrance read: "Exhibit of Largest Known Naturally Occurring Carbon Allotrope (Studious Viewings Only—Gawking Strictly Prohibited)."

Sarah and Mick had arrived on Planet Archimedes in the dead of night and under the cover of a counterfeit research mission. According to Praiseworthy, who recounted the history of Planet Archimedes in extensive detail, the planet had been of keen interest to scientists because it had some of the strangest cloud formations ever observed, its rivers ran in perfectly straight lines, and most importantly, its insects were both plentiful and ugly. Archimedes soon became a scientist's haven. They erected elaborate museums full of complicated interactive exhibits, placed massive jars with holes in the lids in public squares to display Archimedes' most spectacularly ugly insects, and raced to outdo each other by wearing the latest in lab coat and loafer fashion.

When the discoverers of the Dragon's Eye decided to donate it to science, they placed it in the care of Planet Archimedes, whose scientists dropped it several times and then nearly destroyed it during a scientific experiment to determine whether it could be destroyed by a really huge laser beam. (Their conclusion: It could not be destroyed by a laser, but more tests were needed before the theory could be called a fact. All present agreed, however, that the laser was extremely awesome.) The scientists of Archimedes placed the Dragon's Eye in one of their many museums, awaiting further scientific inquiry.

Mick had insisted that they get a full night's rest so their senses would be sharp. He also dismissed Sarah's initial attempts at helping plan the heist, telling her that she couldn't possibly match his expertise in the buccaneer vocation, which sent her into a fit of volcanic rage. In the aftermath of their argument Mick grudgingly allowed her to help with the planning. They would break in shortly before the museum opened. Sarah would be responsible for external distraction, but Mick steadfastly refused to cede any control once they were inside, telling her, "I've been planning this for years." He managed to resist Sarah's subsequent anger, threats, and blackmail.

As they stood carefully behind a wall near the museum, Sarah's heart raced. She and Mick were actually going to steal the Dragon's Eye. Two scientists in white lab coats stood guard outside. A steady stream of pedestrians wearing lab coats moved past the entrance, occasionally bumping into one another when they stared into the sky trying to spot abnormal cloud formations or looked downward to examine interesting insects on the sidewalk with magnifying glasses. Mick had his mechanical duck under his arm, which was Sarah's contribution to the plan.

Mick peeked around the corner again and said, "Okay. Time to move. This had better work."

Mick stepped around the corner and let the duck loose. It slowly waddled toward the guards, and Sarah held her breath, hoping it would distract them. She couldn't even think about how horrible it would be to have Mick lording any failure over her. The scientists were both lost in thought and even though the duck was quacking very loudly, it wasn't until it bumped into one of them that they noticed its presence.

"What's this?" the guard said. "Why, I've seen nothing like it before. It walks like my mother! I shall call it *Harrietus Walkalitus* in the *Aves* order." He picked it up and admired its movements. "What a fine specimen."

"How dare you name the species?" the other guard said. "I saw it seven nanoseconds before you, and if I'm not mistaken, it is a member of a genus I already discovered last weekend on a forest expedition. My research paper is undergoing peer review as we speak! It is truly groundbreaking."

A pedestrian who had been walking by noticed the duck and asked if she could perform an immediate dissection, which caused a slapping fight to break out among the guards. Amid the awkward commotion, no one noticed two children slipping quietly into the museum.

"It worked! It worked! I told you it would work!" Sarah whispered as she hurried through the entrance. "Score one for women! We are so much smarter and—"

Mick grabbed her and stopped her from taking another step.

"Don't touch me, you miscreant, I—"

"Shhhh! Scientists make terrible guards. But they love surveillance equipment." He nodded at a camera on a far wall and pointed at a laser beam that Sarah was about to step into. "Some of these tiles are linked to a central alarm system. They have infrared heat imaging and lots and lots of complicated booby traps. You just about blundered your way into jail."

Sarah shook herself free from Mick, but she stepped behind him. "Fine. You go first."

The main hall of the museum soared high into the air, and paintings of scientific equations filled the walls. In the center of the rotunda was a huge fossilized skeleton of a fearsome extinct monster attacking another fearsome extinct monster. Scattered around them, and much smaller, were a few ancient human skeletons posed with their hands raised in extreme fright. A hologram above the display read: "Nature is not friendly."

Mick carefully sidestepped along the wall of the rotunda until he found a small indentation on the wall. He tapped it twice, and part of the wall slid open with a hiss, revealing a tiny room. He nodded to Sarah and they slipped inside.

The room was a supply closet, but rather than holding cleaning supplies, it was full of extension cords and six-prong adapters. They were knotted and tangled and plugged into one another haphazardly. And the entire mess was emanating from a single plug.

Sarah couldn't believe her eyes. "They have every-thing plugged into one outlet?!"

Mick climbed over the cords and pulled the single plug. They were plunged into darkness. "They're a lit-tle absentminded."

Sarah couldn't see anything, and her racing heart skipped a beat when she had the sudden image of Mick Cracken trying to kiss her in the darkness. Of all the people she wanted to be stuck in a dark closet with in the entire universe, Mick Cracken was surely the very last on the list. She would have rather kissed a snake or a rodent or a porcupine. She heard him scrambling over the cords, felt him brush up against her, and she could hear him breathing, but she couldn't see him. She panicked and put up her fists, and said, "Mick Cracken, you had better not—"

Mick opened the closet door and suddenly Sarah could see again. She slowly put down her dukes. "Oh."

Mick gave her a wry smile, followed by his best in-nocent expression. "I'd better not what? Getting ideas, Sarah Daisy?"

Sarah pushed Mick against the wall and jabbed her finger against his throat. "No one calls me that."

Mick blanched and nodded.

Sarah let him go and they ran through the dark museum, past fearsome taxidermy of animals Sarah

Daisy had never seen before, past interactive displays on the theory of relativity and Planck's Constant, past the exhibit on the history of humankind's unending quest for knowledge. They were almost to the back of the museum, so close to the Dragon's Eye and the wish that would send her and Jacob and Dexter back to Earth.

That was when Sarah heard the scientist's shout.

CHAPTER 19

Jacob Wonderbar stirred awake from a long-needed slumber and tried to remember where he was. He wasn't at home in his bed, he wasn't aboard Lucy or Praiseworthy . . . he felt the soft ground beneath him, and it came back to him in a flash. Numonia.

He quickly sat up and found himself staring straight into the eyes of Moonman McGillicutty.

Jacob screamed.

Moonman yelled, "Ahh! They're awake! They're awake!! Oh, thank the Tree of Life, they're awake!" Moonman McGillicutty danced an awkward jig around the hut. He bumped into a wall and a bit of Numonian dust came sprinkling down.

Dexter sat up and rubbed his head.

Stargirl McGillicutty rushed into the hut with tears in her eyes. "They're awake? Oh, they're awake!! Praise the Tree of Life, we were worried sick! Do you boys realize you slept nearly five hundred days?" She sniffed. "Five hundred whole days! We didn't know if you'd ever wake up." She started sobbing uncontrollably.

"Now, now," Moonman said, giving Stargirl a hug. "The important thing is that . . ."

Night came and Moonman and Stargirl promptly fell asleep.

"These people scare me," Dexter whispered.

"We have to get out of here," Jacob said.

"How long is five hundred Numonia days?"

"Um . . . seven or eight hours, I think."

Dexter shook some dust out of his hair. "This place is nuts."

Moonman and Stargirl woke up and stretched. Stargirl resumed crying.

Moonman said, "Boys, we'd like to host you for a celebratory banquet. You must be starving!"

Dexter and Jacob looked at each other and nodded. Jacob could feel his stomach ache at the thought of eating some food.

Ten Numonian days later, Dexter and Jacob found themselves at a large banquet table with the entire population of the planet. Along with the McGillicuttys were a wrinkled couple named the Bartholomews, who Moonman said in a loud whisper were 352 years old and "don't hear so good," and the Goslings and their seven children, who were all staring at Jacob and Dexter with befuddled expressions.

Jacob and Dexter stared down at their plates, which were both piled high with Numonian dirt shaped into pyramids.

Moonman broke the top off his pyramid and chewed heartily. "Mmm! Stargirl, you've outdone yourself."

She winked at the boys. "Isn't Numonian dirt something? You just pick it up off the ground, form it into a little clump, and eat it! Plus it has so much moisture, we don't even need to drink water." She patted her large belly and leaned over to whisper, "It's so good I just can't help myself sometimes."

Jacob smiled at the Numonians and muttered "Eat it" to Dexter without moving his lips.

"You first," Dexter said.

"No way."

Dexter looked around at the expectant faces of the Numonians and tried to decide whether his fear of disappointing his hosts or his fear of eating disgusting space dust was the more powerful feeling. The situation was growing more awkward by the second as everyone silently waited for them to eat their food. He felt the stirrings of hyperventilation.

"Well?" Stargirl asked eagerly.

Dexter swallowed against his dry throat, his eyes watering. He broke off a tiny piece and stared at it. Hands shaking, he gingerly placed it on his tongue. When he realized he hadn't died instantly, he tentatively chewed and swallowed it, and then smiled through tears at the Numonians, who gave a rousing cheer. Then night fell and everyone went to sleep.

"What does it taste like?" Jacob whispered.

Dexter shrugged. "Better than your mom's tuna surprise."

Jacob stared back at the plate. "That's not saying much."

Jacob quickly put a tiny morsel of food into his mouth, chewed, and swallowed. It tasted like grainy rice that had been ground up and sent through a processor that stripped it of any flavor whatsoever. He felt little bits of Numonian dirt stick in his teeth and he suppressed a gag. He knew he would never be able to finish it, no matter how hungry he was. He did have to admit, however, that it was definitely better than his mom's tuna surprise.

Jacob felt the wind gust that meant morning was

coming. He quickly dumped the rest of his plate onto the ground and stomped it down.

"What are you doing?" Dexter elbowed him. "Why won't you . . ."

Everyone woke up and said their good mornings, but one of the Gosling children gasped and pointed at Jacob Wonderbar's plate.

Moonman's eyes were big. "Young man, you ate your whole plate?"

Jacob smiled and said, "I sure did, and my compliments to the chef!"

Tears formed in Stargirl's eyes. "Oh dear," she said.

Old man Bartholomew shouted, "Is this kid nuts?"

Jacob forced a smile. "I really liked it."

Moonman clasped his hands together. "Oh no. This is all my fault. I should have warned him!" He smacked his head. "Oh no, oh no, oh no . . ."

Jacob looked around the table. "Warned me about what?"

Moonman turned to Jacob, his face creased with worry. "Numonian dirt is meant to be eaten slowly, over the course of many days. If you eat an entire plate at once, it congeals and passes through your intestines in one big lump, and . . ."

"And what?"

Moonman looked at the sky in agony. "And you could burst!"

Jacob's face felt fuzzy. His stomach was certainly growling, but that was because it was empty, not because he was in danger of congealed space dust exploding his intestinal tract. But he couldn't tell the Numonians that he had dumped their beloved dirt on the ground without eating it. He tried to steady his voice. "Oh, I'm sure it will be fine."

"Happened to me in 7823," old man Bartholomew shouted. "It was an ugly scene, son. Ugly! Worst day of my life. It smelled like . . ."

Night came, and the Numonians fell asleep. After a moment of quiet, Moonman had a nightmare and cried out in his sleep. Jacob looked around at the sleeping faces, all locked in anguished expressions, many of them twitching and having a fitful night.

"You have to tell them the truth," Dexter whispered.

"I can't!" Jacob said. "They would be so upset."

"So? Better that than having them think you're going to die."

"I can't do it."

"Wonderbar!"

"No!"

Morning rose and Moonman overslept a little before waking up and rubbing his eyes. "I had the most terrible dream, and . . ." He looked at Jacob's plate. "Oh. It's true."

Stargirl stood up from the table. "We have to get him off Numonia. To a hospital."

Moonman nodded. "Our only hope is the spaceship Swift. Boys, we've never tried to leave Numonia because, you know, why would anyone want to, but by golly, if it will save our little friend here that's what we must do."

Moonman and Stargirl started bounding toward the spaceshift Swift. Dexter kicked Jacob under the table, but he didn't pay any attention.

"Did they say 'leave Numonia'?" Jacob jumped up and ran after them.

Dexter got up and chased after Jacob, who was up to his same old tricks in outer space. Dexter knew very well that Jacob's plans inevitably landed them in trouble, and this time they were in space, they were on their own, and their parents weren't there to rescue them. Dexter had to put a stop to it. It was time for him to tell the Numonians the truth.

"Wait, wait!" Dexter said. After a couple seconds he caught up with them. "Listen to me. Jacob is . . ."

Night fell and Moonman and Stargirl fell asleep.

"Don't you dare say anything," Jacob said. "This is our chance to get off this crazy planet!"

"It's not right, Wonderbar. You can't lie to them."

"Don't. Say. Anything," Jacob said quietly, stepping toward Dexter and poking him in the chest. "I'm not going to let you blow this like you usually do."

Dexter stumbled back in shock. In all their years of friendship Jacob had defended him so many times, but he had never once tried to actually fight or intimidate him. Jacob was his best friend. On another day, on Planet Earth, Dexter would have walked straight out the door and gone home until Jacob apologized. But they were billions of miles away and there might not have even been an Earth to run home to.

Dexter reached down and grabbed some Numonian dust, clumped it together, and threw it at Jacob. "Fine!" he yelled. He stomped away in the opposite direction.

Jacob started to call after Dexter, but instead he let him go. The Numonian space dust had given them a golden opportunity to leave Numonia and reunite with Sarah, and getting off Numonia was more important than Dexter's feelings. Dexter would come around to his plan.

The spaceship Swift was their only shot.

oonman stared at the controls of the spaceship Swift, his hands uncertainly hovering
over the buttons and dials. Jacob and Stargirl stood
behind him, watching to see if he could get the old ship
to lift off. The cockpit of the Swift looked like an antique compared to Lucy's and Praiseworthy's consoles,
and some of the lights inside flickered and sputtered.
Numonian dust filled nooks and crannies. Jacob wasn't
sure the tub of steel and glass would ever be able to lift
off into space again.

"Now, let's see here," Moonman said. "I think my
grandfather told me to . . ." He pressed a button and
stood up quickly, rubbing his backside. "Nope. Seat
warmer."

Jacob looked over at poor Moonman, trying so

desperately to get him off Numonia, all because they thought his insides were going to burst with space dust. They were so worried, and all for nothing. And what if Moonman wasn't a good enough pilot to get back home? What if he fell asleep and flew the spaceship Swift into an asteroid?

Jacob nervously tapped his foot. He wasn't in the habit of admitting when he hadn't told the truth, but the deception had gone far enough. He blurted out, "It was a lie."

Moonman shook his head. "No, son, that really was the seat warmer button, and I just wish—"

"I didn't eat the food. I made it up, and I dumped it on the ground, and I'm so sorry that I made you so worried."

Jacob winced as he awaited their reply. He couldn't even imagine what they would think of him now that they knew the truth.

Stargirl stared at him in confusion. "You didn't eat the food?"

"No, ma'am."

Moonman stood up and peered into Jacob's face. "Son, do you know what this means?"

Jacob shook his head and swallowed nervously.

"It means you can stay on Numonia!" Moonman and Stargirl let out a whoop and began dancing around the spaceship Swift, raising their fists and chanting, "Numonia! Numonia! Numonia!"

Jacob tried to smile, but when he saw their excitement he knew it meant that the spaceship Swift would never fly off the planet. They wouldn't try to leave and he would be stuck on Numonia forever. They loved their planet so much, and it made him miss nice green and brown Earth, which suddenly felt so far away. It may have been a planet filled with detentions and principals and interminable groundings, but it was still his home and he wanted to go back and make sure it was safe.

They heard a loud whooshing noise outside the ship and Moonman whispered, "Shhh." He cocked his head and said, "I've never . . ." And then night came and he fell asleep.

In the Numonian darkness, Jacob walked to the rear of the spaceship Swift, the nighttime stars shining through the portholes. He opened the hatch door, stepped out, and saw one of the most wonderful sights he had ever seen in his life: the lights of the spaceship Lucy, a soft glow shining through the dome of the cockpit, the cargo door open and Dexter standing there waiting for him in the hold. Jacob nearly fainted with relief. Lucy, the ship that had taken them so far from home, had come back for him. His mind raced with what would now be possible. He could leave Numonia and try and find a way home. Moonman and Stargirl could stay on Numonia, and they didn't have to fly the spaceship Swift.

The winds stirred, the sun rose. Moonman and Stargirl woke and stood beside Jacob, looking at Lucy with their arms around each other.

Moonman grabbed Jacob's shoulder with one of his strong hands.

"Son, I want you to know something. You're probably going to leave us now, and I think Stargirl and I both know it. And that's because where you come from is special to you. It may not be as good as Numonia, but it's your home and you'll love your home no matter what. No one can take it away from you."

Jacob looked up into Moonman's and Stargirl's twinkling eyes. "I don't even know if I have a home to go back to," he said quietly.

Moonman smiled. "Well, whatever happens, I just want you and Dexter to know that you'll always have a home on Numonia."

Jacob said, "Thank you," and hugged them. They felt like his grandparents, soft and warm and kind, and he felt a pang of sadness and anger that his dad wasn't even there for him as much as the Numonians had been.

He made his way over to Lucy and climbed aboard,

taking a deep cleansing lung full of air that didn't smell like burp breath. As the cargo door closed he turned back to say one last good-bye to Numonia, but the sun set, night fell, and Moonman and Stargirl were fast asleep.

"Sarah!" Jacob turned and shouted as Lucy blasted off into the sky. "Sarah! Where is she? I knew she'd come back for us!"

Dexter shook his head. "She's not here."

"What?"

"It's just me. Lucy showed up out of nowhere, so I hopped on board and told her where to find you."

"I don't understand."

Dexter shrugged and handed Jacob a ration bar. Jacob tore into it, and as he was chewing he suddenly remembered their fight.

"Thanks for coming back for me," Jacob said.

Dexter stared at the wall for a long time before answering. "That's what friends do."

"You were right, Dexter."

Dexter gave him a shaky grin, "Aw, you know. It happens once in a while."

"Children," Lucy said, "as much as I am enjoying this excruciating display of emotion, I need to know where I should set my coordinates."

"I missed you, Lucy!" Jacob shouted. "Thank you for coming for us."

"Oh dear, well, I suppose I'd rather be commanded by you lunatics than be held captive by a bore of a spaceship, but don't let that go to your heads."

Dexter said to Jacob, "Let's find Sarah and get home."

"Lucy," Jacob said. "Can you take us to Sarah? Where is she?"

Lucy didn't speak for a moment. "I can get you there quickly," she said. "But I don't think you're going to like it."

CHAPTER 21

Sarah heard the scientist's shout just as they rounded a corner and ran directly into his large belly. He was huge, and his massive white lab coat could have covered a horse. His skin was ghostly white and he was wearing mechanical binoculars that covered his eyes and were constantly expanding and retracting.

"Halt!" he cried, waving his head around trying to see the children. "Wait. Back up. I can't see you. This is just a prototype." His binoculars retracted. "Oh. That's better. Now, don't move! I have you in my sights, and . . . why . . . Mick Cracken! I should have known it would be you."

Sarah rolled her eyes, knowing that Mick's ego was pumping up like a balloon.

"We're here to steal the Dragon's Eye," Mick said with a confident smile.

The giant scientist smiled right back and took a menacing step toward the children. He readjusted his binoculars. "I do not think that is within the realm of probable outcomes."

Sarah could tell Mick didn't have a plan for this. He had just waltzed them in and thought he could steal the Dragon's Eye without any difficulty whatsoever, and now that they were caught by a scientist, they really would end up in an interplanetary jail.

"You are under arrest and you may be placed under a slide for microscopic evaluation."

The scientist stepped closer, his huge gnarled hands reaching out toward them. Sarah flinched and prepared to scream.

"One side twenty-eight meters, one side sixty-eight meters, what's the hypotenuse of a right triangle?" Mick shouted.

The scientist stopped, his face turning red. "What . . . what did you say?"

"One side twenty-eight meters, one side sixty-eight meters, what's the hypotenuse of a right triangle?"

The scientist's hands started shaking. "But that's . . . Why, that would require the Pythagorean Theorem. That's . . . that's my favorite mathematical equation!"

The scientist looked at the children.

He looked over at a nearby chalkboard.

He looked at the children. A few quiet seconds passed.

And he ran over to the chalkboard. He furiously started scratching out numbers.

"Go! Go!" Mick shouted.

Sarah stared in disbelief as the scientist worked on the problem. Mick grabbed her by the arm, and she followed after him.

They rounded a corner and screeched to a halt. A small lab mouse rose up from the marble floor of the museum and raised its claws and bared its teeth. The mouse must have thought it was an intimidating gesture, but it couldn't have known that Sarah wasn't scared of mice in the slightest. In fact, she found this one darling and rather dignified.

"Ahh!" Mick yelled. "Mouse! Oh please oh please no." He raised his hands in surrender.

"It's just a mouse! What in the world is wrong with you?" Sarah peered closer at the mouse and saw a small yellow piece of metal on its head. "Is that a crown?"

Mick's entire body was rigid and his eyes were squeezed shut. "They worship those . . . beasts on this planet. They are allowed to roam free when they're not participating in experiments, and everyone is supposed to bow and pay their respects. Oh please oh please. Is it looking at me? I think it's looking at me."

Sarah stared at the mouse and smiled. It was so cute and regal. She bent down and said, "Hi little guy, I'm—"

The mouse launched itself at Sarah's head. Its claws dug in upon impact, and it began running over her scalp, pricking her head like a hundred small needles.

"Ahh!!" she shrieked.

"I told you!" Mick yelled.

Sarah reached for the mouse but it grabbed a piece of her hair and swung down so that it was right in front of her eyes. She screamed and swiped at it, but it jumped onto her shoulder. She heard a small voice say, "I command you to leave at once!" Sarah froze, wondering for a moment if she had only imagined this violent mouse talking or if it had really ordered her to leave. Her mind raced. If the mouse could talk, that meant it was intelligent, and if it was intelligent . . .

"One side twenty-eight meters, one side sixty-eight meters, what's the hypotenuse of a right triangle?"

The mouse stopped scurrying and clung to her back.

"One side twenty-eight meters, one side sixty-eight meters, what's the hypotenuse of a right triangle?" she said again.

She felt the mouse pause for a few seconds. Then

she felt it run down her leg. It scurried up to the chalk-board, grabbed a piece of chalk, and worked on the problem along the bottom of the chalkboard. The scientist watched the mouse start its calculations and realized he had made an error. He erased his work and started over again.

Mick's mouth hung open for a moment. "I'm impressed," he said finally.

"Not much time," Sarah said with a smile. She ran on ahead into the exhibit, and . . .

There it was. The Dragon's Eye. It glittered and glinted in the light that streamed through the large windows into the museum. It was bigger than a car, it was sparkling and brilliant and incredible. Sarah ran over to it, pressed her face against it, and smiled. It felt cool and diamond-y and it was their ticket home. She couldn't wait to see the expression on Jacob's face when he saw that she'd gotten the Dragon's Eye and wished them all to safety.

"Now I just have to call Praiseworthy and we can get out of here." Mick stepped toward a window and talked into a small piece of black plastic. "Come in, Praiseworthy. We have it and we deactivated the alarms. Let's get out of here. I'm sending the coordinates."

Sarah pressed her hand against the Dragon's Eye. She closed her eyes.

"Praiseworthy, come in. Praiseworthy, do you read?" Mick began pacing.

Sarah took a deep breath. "I wish I were back on Earth with Jacob and Dexter," she whispered. She swelled with pride and readied herself to be whisked through the universe at astonishing speeds.

Slowly, she opened her eyes and saw Mick Cracken staring at her. She was still on Planet Archimedes.

Her heart skipped a beat. Maybe she couldn't wish herself back to Earth because Earth didn't exist anymore. She closed her eyes and tried again. "I wish Jacob and Dexter were here with me right now." She opened her eyes. No Jacob and Dexter. "Nothing happened! How does this thing work?"

Mick scratched his head. "Oh. Uh . . . About that . . ."

CHAPTER 22

Jacob and Dexter stared at a building shaped like a giant beaker on a strange planet called Archimedes, where Lucy said they would find Sarah. The planet was full of scary insects and people wearing white lab coats. Jacob peered at the banner in front of the building, which declared that the museum contained the world's largest carbon allotrope.

"What in the heck is a carbon allotrope?" Jacob asked.

Dexter stared at the pedestrians in front of the building, who were bowing before a mouse that was sunning itself on the sidewalk. The mouse seemed oblivious to the attention, but everyone who passed by stopped to pay their respects.

"You know, Earth is actually a very normal planet," Dexter said. "I never thought I'd say that."

Jacob and Dexter shrugged their shoulders, walked over and bowed to the mouse, and then tried to catch the attention of the guards in front of the museum, who were engaged in a spirited conversation.

"Excuse me . . ." Jacob said.

The guard thrust a mechanical duck into his hands. "Ah, good, an impartial observer. Tell me, young man of science. Does this look like a *Harrietus Walkalitus* or a *Liliputus Ricktogramus*?"

"He is hardly an impartial observer," the other guard said. "As I have been trying to tell you, we must establish an independent control group to establish the margin of error, after which we can . . ."

"Have you seen a small blond girl around here?" Dexter asked. "Probably not wearing a lab coat? Sometimes has an attitude problem?"

The guards shook their heads and kept arguing. Jacob suddenly noticed that the duck looked familiar. "Dexter," Jacob said. "Don't you think that duck looks like it belongs to *Mickus Crackenus*?"

Dexter's eyes widened in recognition.

"Oh!" the first guard shouted. "Now don't you go trying to claim credit. As I have repeatedly asserted, I saw it first, and the first scientist who sees a new species gets to name . . ."

"I saw it first . . ." the other guard said. He lunged for the duck, but the first guard slapped his hand away.

"What's in the museum?" Jacob asked.

The first guard sighed and pointed at the banner.

"I know what the sign says, but what's a carbon allotrope?"

"Ha!" the guard laughed. "Ha-ha! He doesn't know what a carbon allotrope is."

"Ha-ha . . ." the other said. "He probably couldn't even get an A plus in multi-planar geometric physics."

"He probably needs a spectrograph transometer to calculate his electromagnetic pulse trajectories."

Jacob clenched his fists, but remembered that he needed to be patient. The first guard rolled his eyes and spoke very slowly. "You might know it as a diamond. Diamond? Yes? Comprehend?"

Jacob's heart raced. If a carbon allotrope was a diamond, that meant the museum held . . . the universe's largest diamond. The Dragon's Eye. Sarah must have been trying to steal it.

Jacob and Dexter ran into the museum.

"Hey," the first guard shouted. "The museum has not yet opened!" The second guard used the distraction to grab the duck, and they tumbled to the ground in a heap, grappling for control.

The museum was dark on the inside save for the little bit of light that came through the entrance, which made the monster skeletons cast huge shadows on the far wall. Jacob had a very bad feeling. What if something went wrong when Sarah was trying to steal the Dragon's Eye? If she had gotten caught or arrested or hurt stealing the Dragon's Eye . . . Jacob started running.

Dexter stopped near the entrance and hesitated. He had liked the idea of going after the Dragon's Eye and wishing for a million wishes, but not when it entailed actually breaking into a museum with crazy guards. They could get into much bigger trouble than he had ever anticipated. Dexter's heart raced. "Wonderbar!"

Jacob turned back in exasperation. "Come on! We have to find her!"

Dexter crossed his arms nervously. "I don't think this is a good idea. What if they think we're trying to steal the Dragon's Eye? We could get arrested."

"We don't have time to discuss this!"

"There's a better way to do this."

"Come on! Don't be such a chicken."

Dexter leaned forward in anger. "You are always

getting me into trouble!" he yelled, his words echoing around the rotunda. "I'm not going any farther."

They stared at each other for a tense moment before Jacob turned and stomped away toward the Dragon's Eye exhibit, furious that Dexter had chickened out yet again. Dexter was always so worried about getting into trouble that he never stopped to thank Jacob for helping him have any fun at all. Dexter never appreciated any of it, not even that he walked home safely most days because of Jacob's protection. And now he was too scared to even help find one of his best friends.

Jacob heard frantic voices as he reached the rear of the museum. One of the voices sounded like Sarah's. He turned a corner, and had to shield his eyes from the glare of a massive diamond.

"I can't believe you lied to me!" Sarah shouted, pointing a finger in Mick's face. "How could you do that? You swore on your buccaneer's honor!"

"Buccaneers don't have any honor!"

Jacob tried to make sense of what he was seeing. "Sarah, what . . . what are you doing here?"

Sarah swallowed and stood for a second in shock. She pointed at the Dragon's Eye as if it were an explanation. "Well, he lied to us." She tried to make her voice sound confident, but it wavered a bit. "This stupid diamond doesn't grant any wishes."

Jacob scowled. "Why didn't you come back for us? Do you realize what this jerk did? We could have been stuck on that planet forever! I told you he was lying!"

Sarah shrunk back a little bit, but Jacob didn't feel any sympathy. She deserved to feel guilty for trusting a stupid space pirate more than her own friend.

A loud alarm suddenly sounded throughout the museum, and the lights turned on. Security cameras swiveled around quickly until they settled on the children, and darts began firing from the walls. A floor tile nearby fell into the basement, and laser beams shot out from every corner. A mechanical voice shouted, "Intrusion! Intrusion!"

"Wonder-something, look out!" Mick shouted.

Jacob turned, but too late, because he felt a firm hand on his shoulder.

Mick ran toward an emergency exit, where a metal gate was slowly lowering.

"Sarah, come on!"

Sarah looked over at Mick. She looked back at Jacob. He was struggling against the scientist's grasp. Suddenly Mick ran back and grabbed her and pulled her away.

"Let go of me!" Sarah shouted.

"Come on! We have to get out of here!"

She finally relented as he pulled her toward the door, and they slid under just before it closed.

"No!" Jacob yelled. "No, no, no!!"

The scientist spun him around, and Jacob saw that he had retractable binoculars over his eyes and chalk dust all over his hands and lab coat.

"Hold on, I can't see you," the scientist said, fiddling with the controls for his binoculars. "I . . . There you are. What . . . You're wearing a disguise? Well, Mick Cracken, very clever, but I have you now."

"I'm not Mick Cracken!" Jacob said. "Let me go."

"A likely story. I have one thing and just one thing to say to you right now."

Jacob gulped and braced himself.

"The hypotenuse is seventy-three point five three nine one zero five two four three four zero one meters."

Jacob tried to make sense of what he had just heard.

"Also, you're under arrest."

CHAPTER 23

Every step Sarah took sunk her further and further into despair. She and Mick were running away from the museum, through a park with rolling green hills and colorful wildflowers, which was littered with giant, elaborate ant farms and talking statues that recited scientific equations. The air was filled with ugly flying insects, and they had to dodge scientists running around haphazardly with butterfly nets.

Sarah had left Jacob behind twice. Twice! She couldn't forget the hurt look on his face. He would never, ever forgive her. She felt so guilty and selfish for saving herself just as he was caught by the scientist. She suddenly stopped running, unable to go any farther. She couldn't even imagine how much Jacob must have hated her. She was so embarrassed at how wrong she had been.

"Hey!" she yelled. "Hey, jerk! We have to go back."

"We can't go back! We have to keep running. If we get caught, that's it."

Sarah felt a lump forming in her throat. "But . . . we can't just leave him there!"

Mick beckoned for her to keep going. "He'll be fine."

Sarah sat down in the grass and felt her eyes fill with tears. She tried to stop them. She needed to be strong and smart, not hysterical and weak. Crying was such a girly thing to do, and it wasn't at all how she wanted to conduct herself. "I'm too strong to cry," she said as the tears began streaming down her face.

Mick sat down beside her.

"I hate you," she cried. "I hate you for lying to me. I can't believe I didn't go back for him. He would never, ever have done what I did. Never in a million years. I feel so terrible."

She pounded the soft grass with her hand. "He's never going to forgive me." She wiped tears away from her cheek. "And I don't even blame him."

They watched as a scientist ran past them, chasing after a hopping serpent. "He'll forgive you," Mick said.

Sarah glared at Mick. "Why would he?" Her voice caught. "I wouldn't forgive me. I'd hate me." She began sobbing again.

Mick's voice was quiet and he dropped all attempts at being a cocky space pirate. "Because you are really good friends. And that's how it works. It's all my fault anyway. You guys just weren't very excited about stealing the Dragon's Eye, so I made up the thing about the wish. And we were so close! If only Praiseworthy had come in time, we would have had it and—"

"I don't care about your stupid diamond!" Sarah stared at the horizon through her tears. She missed her parents and her cat, Susan B. Anthony, and her older sister, whom she never got to see ever since she moved away to college. She even missed The Brat. They might have all been gone because of the space kapow, and she didn't even have a diamond to wish them back.

Mick cleared his throat. "I'm sorry."

Sarah wiped tears away. "We have to go back for Jacob. Right now."

Mick stood up and reached for her hand. "It's too dangerous to go back right now. Let's go find Praiseworthy. Then we can come up with a plan."

She looked up at Mick and though the sight of his face filled her with rage, Sarah knew she didn't have much choice but to go along with him. He had the spaceship and she didn't know the first thing about rescuing someone from a bunch of crazy scientists. If she was going to save Jacob she would need his help.

She refused his outstretched hand and got up on her own. "Fine. Let's go," she said.

They ran to the far end of the park, where Praiseworthy was sitting peacefully in a meadow. Sarah exhaled with happiness when she saw his dainty exterior and shoddy black paint job. They ran through the cargo door and Sarah went into the bedroom with the plush bed and jumped straight onto it. She was so tired. But she had work to do. She had to figure out how to save Jacob Wonderbar.

"Praiseworthy!" she shouted. "I missed you."

"Oh, Mistress Daisy," Praiseworthy said mournfully. "You shouldn't have come back."

Sarah sat straight up. "What?"

She heard a commotion in the hold and she ran to the door and flung it open. Ten men wearing red spacesuits with gold crowns printed on their chests and arms were gathered around Mick, who was backed into a corner with his hands raised. Sarah knew immediately they were the royal guards. It was a trap.

Mick saw Sarah and shook his head sadly.

The leader of the guards stepped slowly toward
Mick, his footsteps echoing through the hold. He
looked tough and imposing, and Sarah's breath caught
when he drew close. Then he knelt to one knee in front
of Mick and bowed his head.

"Time to go home, Your Highness."

CHAPTER 24

Jacob struggled against the handcuffs. It was all a huge misunderstanding. He sat restrained in a chair in a huge auditorium, his face projected onto a large screen behind him. The head scientist wore a bright white lab coat and a purple polka-dotted bow tie, and he seemed unduly excited. The floor of the auditorium contained several lab stations, which were piled high with Bunsen burners, beakers, vials, microscopes, and spare computer parts. Every seat in the room was filled. The scientists had brought their favorite calculators and were rowdy with excitement.

Jacob didn't want anything to do with the Dragon's Eye from the very start, and he jerked his wrists with rage when he thought about Dexter refusing to follow him and Sarah running away with the idiot pirate. He wondered if he was really so untrustworthy that his own friends wouldn't believe him. He may have been notorious for misbehaving at school, but he had never once lied to his friends. Well, other than the time he convinced Dexter his skin was going to start glowing in the dark because he swatted a firefly.

"This trial will be conducted by scientific method!" the head scientist said. "You all know the procedure, and we will uphold accuracy and exacting reason. We are men and women of science, and we will behave as such. Is there a hypothesis?"

A young scientist with thick glasses stood up. "Did you know that if you type the number 5318008 into your calculator and turn it upside down, it spells 'boobies'?"

The room erupted, papers went flying, and the trial was unanimously suspended for ten minutes as scientists attempted the feat and then elbowed their colleagues, laughing hysterically. The young scientist received many pats on the back and was immediately recommended for a prestigious award.

After the commotion had subsided, the head scientist

once again asked if any of the scientists had a hypothesis.

The giant scientist who had caught Jacob stood up. "My hypothesis is that he is Mick Cracken in disguise! Although he might be a girl. There was a girl with Cracken too. My hypothesis is that he's either Mick Cracken or a girl!"

A great hubbub commenced. Jacob knew he needed to speak up before he ended up fried by a Bunsen burner or stuffed into a vat of acid. Surely if he just explained the situation to a group of scientists, they would understand. They might even help him find his way back home through a crack in the space-time continuum.

Jacob had been in the principal's office enough times over the years to have perfected his technique for getting into the least amount of trouble possible. He molded his eyes and eyebrows into the perfect expression of innocence and fear, a face he had practiced for hours in the mirror.

"I'm not a girl," Jacob said reasonably. "And I'm not Mick Cracken. I'm Jacob Wonderbar. I'm from the Planet Earth, and—"

The crowd gasped. "Earth!" a woman shouted. "This is worse than we thought. My hypothesis is that he came to steal the carbon allotrope for those vile Earthers, probably to build a weapon that will kill us all! It's an act of war!"

There were shouts of assent.

Jacob shook his head with a patient smile. "I didn't want to steal anything. I just wanted to find my friends. I didn't even believe the stupid diamond existed."

The head scientist directed his laser pointer straight at Jacob's forehead. "The hypothesis for review is that this Earther, who may or may not be a girl, came to our planet to steal a carbon allotrope in order to start an intergalactic war. How shall we conduct the experiment?"

"Let's turn him over to the space monkeys and let them decide!"

158

"Switch his brain with a lab rat's, then ask the lab rat if he's guilty!"

Jacob imagined waking up in a mouse's body or in a cage with monkeys and knew it was time for hysterics. "Stop!" Jacob shouted. The room immediately quieted. He had to go for broke. He summoned fake tears and sniffed loudly, hoping he was convincing. "I didn't try to steal the dia . . . I mean the carbon allotrope. I was just trying to find my friends! The whole thing wasn't even my idea, it was that stupid buccaneer Cracken's plan. I really didn't do it! I promise!"

"We could shoot him with the really big laser," a woman said. There were murmurs of agreement. Jacob gulped.

"I have it!" said the young scientist who had performed the calculator trick. "The perfect experiment. We should simply present him the allotrope as a gift. If he takes it, clearly it is something he wants and it means he came to our planet to steal it. If he does not take it, it would mean he was innocent. What do you suppose he would do?"

"I don't want it! I'd leave it just to get back to my friends," Jacob said.

The scientist quickly rose to his feet. "Precisely what a thief would say! Who wouldn't take a free carbon allotrope? You'd have to be a madman not to take it.

159

Clearly he has something to hide. Guilty as charged!"

The rest of the scientists rose to their feet to cheer and congratulate their colleague. The head scientist at the front of the class waved his laser pointer around and pointed it at Jacob's heart.

"I knew you were guilty," he whispered cheerfully.

Jacob struggled against his restraints, trying one last time to break free. Now that they had found him guilty, he knew the next step would be to decide his punishment.

The head scientist signaled for silence and said, "Now then. We must analyze our results and move to our conclusion. Clearly this Earth human has demonstrated his intent to steal our precious carbon allotrope in order to start a war. However, as we all know, this is just a theory. The experiment must be independently verified through experiments on other Earthers before it is accepted as scientific fact. The subject shall be placed under proper supervision until we find more twelve-year-old Earthers for testing."

"What does that mean?" Jacob asked.

The head scientist giggled. "You will be sent to Planet Paisley for rehabilitation."

Jacob had no idea where Planet Paisley was, and from the sound of the scientist's laugh, he was sure he didn't want to know.

CHAPTER 25

Dexter Goldstein sat in the captain's chair aboard Lucy, all alone and quiet. He stared at the buttons and lights on the pilot's console, trying to decide what he should do. His friends were probably running around the universe looking for each other, but after spending a couple of days in outer space, Dexter knew he wasn't cut out for space-faring. He'd had enough adventure.

Jacob and Dexter were both only children and didn't have any brothers or sisters, but they had known each other since they were babies. Or more accurately, even before they were babies because their moms liked to go shopping for baby supplies together before they were both born. Dexter liked to imagine that he and Jacob had learned their shared hatred of shopping based on those prenatal experiences.

Dexter thought back to the time he and Sarah and Jacob had made a pact in the forest. That night, Jacob hadn't looked at all like the King of the School who picked football teams at recess and planned practical jokes that even made teachers laugh sometimes. Ever since his dad had left, Jacob still ruled the school, but Dexter could tell that something was different about him, even if he and Sarah were the only people who knew him well enough to notice.

Dexter remembered that he looked up at the sky when they all swore they would be there for one another always, and the stars felt so far away, just flaming balls of gas that somehow cast a few random rays of light down on Earth at night. Nothing to get excited about. Yet he knew that Jacob really needed him. It was around that time when Dexter's mom started warning him about his best friend, telling Dexter that he had to stand up for himself, that just because Jacob told him to do something it didn't mean that he had to do it. She said Dexter had to be responsible for them both because Jacob wasn't in a frame of mind to be making positive choices.

At the time Dexter had thought he knew one thing: Jacob really was his brother. They may have had different moms and dads, and in fact Dexter's parents were vaguely terrified of Jacob, but they looked out for each other, they understood each other, and they would have defended each other to the end.

Now his brother had betrayed him. Jacob had landed him in detention yet again, he had bullied him on Numonia, and he wouldn't even listen to him when he went charging off into the museum. He wondered if it really was possible for a brother to act the way he did, and he thought that maybe the stars weren't strong enough to swear on. They couldn't replace blood and family.

Dexter was tired and scared, and he didn't even know the first thing about how to find Jacob and Sarah on some random planet full of crazy scientists. He wanted his parents. He wanted to be at home, where his sock drawer was perfectly organized, where he knew that they would have arugula and goat cheese salad for dinner on Monday and veggie pizza on Friday, and where he had the cleanest aquarium and the healthiest tropical fish anyone had ever seen.

He decided that Jacob and Sarah would have to take care of themselves for a while. He was out of his league. His parents would know what to do, and he needed to find them to get help. He had to see if they were okay. Even if it meant leaving his brother behind.

With a shaky voice, Dexter shouted, "Lucy! Take me back to the space kapow."

Lucy groaned and said, "Little man, I don't think that's such a—"

"Do it!" Dexter yelled.

Lucy was quiet for a moment, then said, "Very well."

As the ship rocketed off Planet Archimedes, Dexter tried to look back for some sign of his friends. But as the planet receded into the distance, he was all alone.

CHAPTER 26

Sarah Daisy and Mick Cracken were trapped in the princess' quarters with a soldier stationed outside the room at all times. The royal guard had taken command of Praiseworthy, and they were headed to the royal planet for a reckoning with Mick's father, who, Sarah suddenly realized, was obviously the king.

"You're really a prince?!" she whispered furiously.

"I don't want to talk about it."

"You're prince of the whole galaxy?"

"Well . . . technically the universe. We've never really found a rival royal family who has challenged us. It's terrible. I hate it more than anything."

Sarah was skeptical and she waited for Mick to laugh, but when he wouldn't look at her, she gathered that he was serious. His shoulders were slumped, his lips were pressed together, and he seemed utterly depressed.

"Why didn't you tell me? And what in the heck is wrong with being a prince?"

"It's not fair! Why should I have to wear a crown and sit on a stupid chair and be waited on hand and foot when all I want to do is go and steal things and have fun? And it's completely corrupt! I believe that rulers should be elected by the people, and in fact, if I had my way I would do away with the whole thing entirely. Democracy!" Mick smacked his fist against his palm for emphasis.

Sarah looked around at the dainty pink room. "So, wait. Praiseworthy is your sister's spaceship? You stole this from your sister?"

Mick sighed. "Don't even get me started on Mistress Silver Spoon."

Sarah looked up at the ceiling, still not knowing whether to really believe it all. "Is this true, Praiseworthy?"

"Oh dear heavens, Mistress Daisy, it is dreadfully true, and I share Master Cracken's dismay that we have been captured. The adventures we might have had together! Although I must say, Mistress Silver Spoon is quite a lovely young lady, and—"

"No she's not!" Mick shouted. "She's horrible and

spoiled and conniving and she doesn't appreciate any-thing!"

"Oh, dear me," Praiseworthy said.

Sarah looked over at Mick, who was staring at the ground, his knees tucked under his chin. His black hair was swept messily into his face and his eyes lacked the spirit of danger and excitement they'd had just a few days ago. Even though nearly everything that she had heard come out of his mouth had been a lie, he seemed rather genuinely devastated about being captured, and she couldn't help but feel a little sorry for him.

She swallowed her anger and decided she could be nice to him in this instance. She could be the bigger person. She reached over and tried to pat Mick on the back, but he scooted away out of her grasp.

"No! Not you too!" Mick shouted, his eyes cold.

"What did I do?"

"You're just like everyone else," he sneered.

"What? What are you talking about?"

"You hated me when I was a pirate and now that you find out I'm a prince, you start acting nice to me? No way. You're just like all of the friends my dad tried to find for me. I'd rather be alone."

Sarah's hand went to her mouth and she had to pause for a moment to make sure she had heard what she thought she had just heard. "That's what you think of me? How shallow do you think I am?"

Mick's lips curled into a snarl. "You pretended you liked me and now you want to take it back. I see right through you."

"Have you lost your mind?"

Mick sat by himself in silence and stared into space.

Sarah did have to admit that she had been somewhat rude to Mick on occasion, but in her defense, he had been quite a toad himself, lying to her about the Dragon's Eye and always bragging about stealing this and coming up with a masterful plan for that. It wasn't as if he had been such a pleasant individual to be around, and he would have to think again if he thought she was going to go gaga over him just because he happened to be a pretend prince of the crazy universe.

She gave up on attempting to be civil to Mick Cracken. She had to plan her escape. She was going to save Jacob Wonderbar.

"Mistress Daisy," Praiseworthy said, "If I might interject, we are nearly at Planet Royale, and your hosts would like to know whether you would prefer to take breakfast in bed or while sunning on a beach. Furthermore, they would like to know your favorite candies and snacks so that your guest suite might be properly stocked with the closest handmade approximations. Lastly, they would like to know your favorite color, as they are arranging an evening gala in your honor and will have a gown prepared for your arrival. They asked me to express their dearest hope that your stay at the palace will be perfectly extraordinary and marvelous."

Mick shook his head with disgust. "I hate this place."

CHAPTER 27

After they finally set their course to Planet Paisley, Jacob began to feel that there was something very strange afoot.

The trip to Planet Paisley aboard a research vessel should have only taken a few hours, but his captor kept getting distracted by fascinating star system formations, and they took several lengthy detours. They passed through an asteroid belt that traced a figure eight around two twin blue planets, saw the impossibly bright, pulsing light of a faraway supernova, and came just close enough to a black hole to feel a slight tug from the intense gravity before they sped safely away. If Jacob hadn't been under arrest he might have actually enjoyed himself.

The first moment that pricked the back of his neck

came when he tried to change the subject from galaxy formations and dark matter to Planet Paisley, and the scientist simply continued with his monologue on the wonders of interplanetary formations.

The second peculiar moment occurred when they entered Planet Paisley's atmosphere and the scientist identified Jacob to the customs authorities as "Antoine Exupery" rather than by his actual name.

"Why didn't you give them my real name?" Jacob asked when they were cleared to land.

"We wouldn't want to alarm the locals."

"What does that mean?" Jacob asked.

The scientist smiled. "It's for your own safety."

"But . . ."

"We will be landing shortly."

They touched down in a park. Jacob stepped onto the grass and turned back to ask the scientist where he should go, but he was greeted by a slamming cargo door and the sounds of a spaceship readying for takeoff.

Jacob darted away and was barely out of range of the rocket boosters when they fired with a fierce blast and the ship rose back up into the atmosphere. As he watched the ship sail away out of sight, Jacob felt a mixture of relief and nervousness. He was finally free of the crazy scientists. But he had a bad feeling about Planet Paisley.

Jacob found the edge of the park and took a look around. Apart from a slightly greenish sky, the street looked like it could have been located in any city on Earth, with a concrete sidewalk and cars streaming down the street. Jacob passed a clothing store that displayed floral print dresses, pointy glasses, and beige clogs in the front window, and another that advertised ten-speed bicycles.

But as he walked down the street, he noticed that there was something strange about the pedestrians. The women wore old dresses and sensible shoes, and they all seemed abnormally tall. The men wore ill-fitting khaki pants and blazers over T-shirts or sweaters that were several sizes too large. Glasses were common, and apparently the thicker the frame, the better. The people all looked vaguely familiar. Jacob had an eerie feeling that he had seen some of them before, but he couldn't place them.

Jacob walked over to a woman who was peering through her glasses at some sheets of papers in a manila folder.

"Excuse me," Jacob said. "I—"

"Why are you not in class, young man?" the woman said.

"I—"

"Where were you when your class was taking roll?"

"Taking roll? I—"

"Say hey there, little fella," said a man wearing a mock turtleneck, navy blazer, khakis, and Birkenstock sandals with white socks. He had his shaggy hair pulled back into a ponytail. "You probably think I'm a square because of my day gig, but did you know that I paint some pretty radical art in my spare time?"

"Young man," the woman said, "you have five seconds to tell me why you are not in class on your own planet. Five . . . four . . . three . . ."

"I don't know what you're talking about!" Jacob yelled.

The woman peered down at Jacob, holding her glasses up to her eyes, and recoiled with a start. "Oh my . . . Do you . . . do you see who this is? It's . . ."

"Who?" the man asked. Then he looked at Jacob more closely and backed up, raising his hands. "Whoa. Back off, kid. Stay away from me."

"Help!!" the woman shouted. "Someone please help! It's Jacob Wonderbar! On our planet! Someone call the principal!"

"How do you know who I am?!" Jacob shouted.

"We've been warned about you," the woman said.

"We've *all* been warned about you," the man said.

Jacob looked around at the women and men on the street wearing out-of-style fashion, and it slowly

dawned on him. The mock turtlenecks. The thin-wheeled ten-speed bicycles. The cardigans. The faint smell of stale coffee.

They were substitute teachers. All of them.

Jacob screamed. The subs screamed.

Jacob started running.

CHAPTER 28

Dexter Goldstein stared out the cockpit window at the Spilled Milky Way galaxy. The universe was just as he and his friends had left it in the aftermath of the giant space kapow: broken. Space was streaked with light and pulsating stars for as far as he could see. The mess was surely many light-years across, and he knew that Earth and his parents and his home were on the other side.

Dexter thought about what had led him to a point in his life where he was flying a spaceship without his friends and had been partially responsible for a colossal interplanetary explosion. He had gone willingly with Jacob and Sarah, he had agreed to spacewalk when he should have insisted that they go straight home, and he had deferred to Sarah when she wanted to steal the Dragon's Eye.

Dexter was tired of being a follower, always letting Jacob get him into trouble, and he imagined remaking himself into a new, confident individual who wasn't scared of disappointing his friends. He would be more like his mom, who always knew what to do and made sure that he and his dad were given proper instructions, using intimidation and force of will if necessary. He would be strong and decisive and powerful. People would fear him. It would be the Era of Dexter.

"Calculate a way through, Lucy," Dexter said in his best captain's voice.

"There's no way through," Lucy said.

"Then calculate a way around."

Lucy sighed. "By the time we made it around and back to Earth, you would be old and gray."

For a moment Dexter wondered what Jacob Wonderbar would do, but then he remembered that Jacob Wonderbar would probably do the first thing that popped into his head and blow them all to bits.

"Go forward!" Dexter shouted.

"Young man . . ."

"I said forward!" Dexter wondered if he was being rude, and his heart began racing with nervousness that he had crossed the line. He hoped that Lucy still liked him. "Um, please?" He furrowed his brow. Did leaders say "please"? Being captain was harder than he thought. He wondered how anyone could make decisions at all when there were feelings to consider. He needed to buy a book on leadership.

"Lucy, are you mad at me?"

"I might be if I weren't so overwhelmingly bored."

"Can you please let me know if you're ever mad at me? I really don't want to have a situation where we're . . ."

Dexter trailed off when he saw flashing lights ahead that weren't cosmic at all but rather looked man-made, or at least Astral-made.

"Please slow down." He wondered if his tone was appropriate, and added, "If that's okay with you."

As they approached the flashing lights, which were affixed to a bulky spaceship, Dexter saw a large man in an orange spacesuit floating in space and holding a red stop sign. Lucy stopped beside him, and the man peered absentmindedly through the window at Dexter.

"Hello?" Dexter said through the intercom. "What's happening?"

"Construction," the man said.

"Do you know if Earth is okay?"

"Earth? No."

"Earth is gone?!" Dexter shrieked.

"'No' as in, no, I don't know if Earth is okay."

"Oh." Dexter took a deep breath. "How long is the construction going to take?"

The construction worker squinted his eyes and thought about it for a while. "Mmmm . . . a project like this, if we work some overtime and assuming material costs don't go too high and we get all the parts we need . . . I'd say you're probably looking at a millennium or two. Give or take."

"A thousand years? Is there a detour?"

"No sir, there is not."

"That's what my spaceship said," Dexter said. "I don't think she likes me."

The construction worker blinked at Dexter. "Uh-huh."

"Are you sure there isn't any possible way through? It's really urgent. I'm not supposed to be in outer space and my parents don't know I'm here." Dexter felt tears forming in his eyes, and he was embarrassed that the construction worker could see them. "I really, really have to go home right now."

"Wow, I'm sorry, kid," the man said. "We'll probably have an alternate route set up in a year or so, but I . . . wish there was something I could do."

"A year?! I can't wait a year!"

"Young man," Lucy said, her voice uncharacteristically soft. "I can't take you home, but I do know about something that could help. There's something called the Looking Glass."

"Yes, the Looking Glass," the construction worker said. "Good idea, spaceship!"

"My name is Lucy," she snapped.

"Oh. Sorry."

"What's the Looking Glass?" Dexter asked.

"It's a mirror you can look into and see anything in the universe. Anything anywhere. You won't be able to talk to your parents or to go Earth, but you might be able to see how they are doing."

"Where is it?"

"Well . . . It's back on Planet Archimedes."

CHAPTER 29

Sarah Daisy awoke from a deep slumber in the perfectly soft sheets and heavy blankets of her bed on Planet Royale. As her eyes slowly began to focus, she stared up at the twenty-foot ceiling painted with murals of stars and spaceships. She had tossed and turned with worry the night before, but had eventually succumbed to sleep. She realized how tired she had been, not only from the stress and chaos of her space voyage, but from the early-morning soccer practices and the piano lessons and the homework and extra-credit homework and all of the other extracurriculars she had to endure so that she would have a bright future and get into a top-tier college.

After a couple of minutes staring at the ceiling, Sarah finally decided that she needed to get up and move around. She put on a robe that had been draped over a magnificent antique chair. As she slipped into it she was suddenly so comfortable she nearly tripped and fell.

She opened the French doors to her terrace and she gasped when she saw the view. She had arrived the night before and was seeing Planet Royale in the daylight for the first time. Her terrace overlooked a beautiful turquoise lagoon surrounded by crystal white sand beaches and exotic green trees. The water stirred and a pink dolphin sailed into the air in a graceful arc before splashing contentedly back down. The splash was followed closely by a smaller dolphin, who leaped into the air and said "Hi!" before landing with a belly flop and heading back beneath the surface.

Sarah's breath caught. She wasn't sure she heard what she thought she heard, and . . .

"Hi!" the baby dolphin shouted when it leaped back above the surface.

"Hi!" Sarah shouted back.

The baby dolphin soared into the air in response and spun in a circle before landing with a splash.

Sarah heard a rap on her doorframe, and she turned and saw her butler, Sven, carrying a platter of food.

He placed waffles and fruit and orange juice on the table. "This is the finest breakfast we could provide on such short notice based on your specifications. Please accept the chef's apologies because the flour in the waffles was made from wheat that was harvested a week ago. I'm really sorry we weren't able to find anything fresher. The fruit was picked this morning rather than minutes ago, as we would normally prefer. For dessert, the chef is currently preparing the finest chocolate the universe has ever known, but he's going to need a bit more time, as he is currently attempting groundbreaking feats of chocolate preparation that will revolutionize dessert forever. He said he'd be finished shortly, but I should warn you that you may faint from the deliciousness and thus you must take great care and eat the chocolate only while sitting down, and furthermore . . ."

"Sven, have you heard anything about Earth?" Sarah asked.

Sven nodded. "Yes, I have. Earth is perfectly fine, Miss Daisy."

"It is?" Sarah wanted to jump for joy, but there was something about Sven's demeanor that made her unsure that she could trust him. Any resident of a royal palace that housed Mick Cracken was surely suspect.

She took a bite of her waffle and squeezed her eyes shut in amazement. It was the softest, most impeccable waffle she had ever tasted. She felt perfectly warm rays of sunshine on her cheeks and she tried to relax for the first time since they blasted off. Sven slipped quietly away.

After a few moments of lying in the sun, Sarah started tapping her finger on the lounge chair. She tried to focus on the soft breeze and the magnificent weather. Then her foot started fidgeting. Her back started itching and she reached around to scratch it. Then she found that she was uncomfortable and flung herself onto her side. Her mind strayed to her upcoming piano recital, and she realized that if Earth still existed, she really needed to practice her sonata, because if she made it home, she needed to please her piano teacher, and she had made a side bet with Jacob that she would win the state competition and . . .

She bolted upright. She had been so caught up celebrating and relaxing, she had stopped planning how to save Jacob Wonderbar. She also realized she was extremely bored.

"Sven?" Sarah called.

He appeared at her side within moments. "Yes, Miss Daisy?"

"I need to leave now."

"I'm afraid that's impossible, Miss Daisy. The king has requested that all children stay on the planet until further notice."

Sarah glared at Sven and her mind raced as she considered what to do. She needed an excuse to wander around and explore so she could find a way to escape. And perhaps get some rehearsing in while she was at it. "Are there any pianos in the palace? I have a big competition coming up and I really need to practice."

Sven beamed. "Miss Daisy, I'm so pleased that you asked about that. When we heard that an Earth girl would be joining us on our planet, we had every piano on the entire planet swiftly sent through the nearest wood chipper so you couldn't possibly be tempted to rehearse. I'm sure you'll agree that their mere existence was a risk we couldn't take. We know how many Earther children are tortured with that infernal instrument. I hope your stay will be filled with nothing but relaxation."

"Relaxation? I can't relax! What in the heck am I supposed to do with myself? I like playing the piano!" Sarah frowned. It was the first time she had ever admitted out loud that she actually enjoyed playing the piano.

Sven backed up a step. "Why . . . Why . . . Shall I schedule an appointment with the royal masseuse?"

"You want me to lie down for half an hour on a board and do nothing?!"

Sarah heard a door slam in her suite, and she turned

and saw Mick Cracken walking in with a beautiful brunette girl about Sarah's age. She wore a blue flowing dress that looked terribly expensive and she had a sparkling tiara in her hair. Sarah clutched her robe around herself. Sven slipped away as they joined her on the terrace.

Mick seemed utterly depressed, and he waved in the girl's direction. "Sarah, Mistress Silver Spoon," Mick mumbled. "Mistress Silver Spoon, Sarah."

"Oh, STOP," the girl said, punching Mick playfully. Her voice was melodious, her eyes were lively, and Sarah thought they might be fast friends. "Isn't my brother Michaelus quite something?"

"Michaelus?" Sarah laughed. "That's your real name?"

Mick closed his eyes and looked as if he were praying to be struck by lightning.

"I'm ever so sorry to barge in on you like this," the girl said. "My name is Princess Catalina Penelope Cassandra Crackenarium. You can call me Princess Catalina, but that's as informal as I can bear." She presented her hand for Sarah to shake.

"Um. Nice to meet you," Sarah said. "Princess Catalina."

"Charmed. Are you finding everything to your liking? I told that rotten chef not to serve you week-old

186

flour, but my orders arrived too late. I hope you weren't forced to spit out your food."

"No, not at all. It was incredible."

"Oh, you silly thing. I've just been dying to meet you. When I heard there was a girl aboard my ship and that she would be joining us for a gala, I had been worried that she might be prettier than me." Catalina looked Sarah up and down. "I needn't have worried, clearly." She burst out laughing.

Sarah laughed as well, but then stopped. "Wait, what?"

"Earthers are just so terribly boring, don't you think? Always yammering about their stress levels and how they need a vacation. Personally, I don't know how you can stand them. You seem passable, I suppose, if a tad on the plain side."

Sarah's ears started burning and she clenched her fists.

"Oh my," Catalina said. "Would you look at that? I've gone and upset her." She laughed. "Oh Sarah dear, we must work on those Earther instincts. I'm going to let you get back to sunning that ghostly pale skin of yours, and you ring me if you need any fashion advice. Mmkay? Ta, darling."

Sarah watched Catalina sashay out the room, and then looked over at Mick, who had his eyebrows raised, waiting for Sarah to tell him that he had been right about his sister. Sarah turned away in a huff. She wasn't going to give that scoundrel the time of day after his performance aboard Praiseworthy.

All the same, she really couldn't believe how Mistress Silver Spoon had treated her. When she found out that Mick Cracken had a princess for a sister, she had never for a second considered the notion that Mick Cracken might actually be the better sibling.

There were some very questionable genetics running through the Crackenarium family.

CHAPTER 30

Jacob ran down the street on Planet Paisley, compiling a mental list of the pranks he had pulled on substitute teachers over the years. He had insisted that substitutes pronounce his last name with a German accent: "Jacob . . . *Voonderbar.*" He had pretended to be a foreign exchange student. He'd convinced one substitute that he was a soccer phenom who didn't have to do his homework because he was leaving to join Manchester United's youth squad. He'd convinced another that Barack Obama was his uncle. He had once faked choking in the middle of class and made Dexter act like he was performing the Heimlich maneuver, which nearly caused the sub to pass out when Jacob spit the peanut that had been "choking" him onto the teacher's desk.

Jacob was quite confident the subs that were chasing him were out for blood.

"Young man!" he heard a woman on the street shout. "Young man, do you have a hall pass?"

"Come back here this instant!" a man shouted. "You'll get detention for this!"

Jacob looked behind him and saw a group of subs running after him, but they were not in good shape and were slowing down. Jacob relaxed his pace as the subs bent over and caught their breath, holding one another up and fanning themselves. He didn't know why he had been so worried.

"Ha-ha! That's Jacob *Voonderbar* to you!" Jacob shouted.

That was when he saw the cavalry.

Two young subs wearing bow ties and thick black glasses swooped into the street aboard two ancient but lively ten-speed bicycles. They were heading straight toward Jacob at an impressive speed and were armed with white earphones, which they had tied into lassoes and were swinging over their heads, preparing to snare Jacob.

Jacob turned around and started running again. The young subs were quickly right behind him. When Jacob looked over his shoulder they were so close that he could see the buttons on their book bags.

They threw some guitar picks in front of Jacob, and he slipped on them but regained his balance and kept running.

Jacob was getting tired. He was no match for these younger subs in their natural habitat. Normally in class they made for some of the easiest foils of all and he was able to distract them permanently off of the lesson plan simply by asking for some good music recommendations. But this was different.

Jacob saw some trees up ahead, and he headed straight toward them, hoping he could lose the subs there.

One of the subs rode up beside him and swung his white lasso around Jacob, pulling him tight and stopping him in his tracks. He tried to move his arms, but he was stuck. The subs screeched to a stop beside him.

"Ah! No! Stop!" Jacob shouted. He racked his brain for his best tactics against young subs. "Are you in a band? What instrument do you play? Can I see your guitar?"

"You're not fooling us this time," the first one sneered. "Jacob *Voonderbar* . . ."

"We are in a band, though," the second one said.

"He's right. It's sort of an emo punk thing, really inaccessible. You probably wouldn't get it."

Jacob swung his hands up and grabbed hold of the

lasso and pulled as hard as he could. The first sub stumbled forward and fell off his bike. Jacob pulled hard again and a small black piece of plastic swung through the air and hit him square in the forehead.

"Ow!"

"My Telly!" the first sub shouted. "No!! Please, not my Telly!"

Jacob shrugged off the lasso and ran toward the trees. The subs got back on their bikes and rode in pursuit.

Jacob reached the first tree, and turned around to see the subs screech to a halt a safe distance away. Jacob blinked in shock. They refused to chase him farther.

"We'll get you!" the first young sub shouted.

"And let us know if you need any music recommendations!" the second one yelled. "I could put together a playlist that would blow your mind."

Then they turned around and rode away.

Jacob leaned against a tree as he caught his breath. He could not for the life of him understand why the subs had suddenly stopped chasing him. Given Jacob's antics over the years, he was surprised they hadn't succeeded in tearing him limb from limb, or at the least captured him and placed him before a spitwad-firing squad.

But whatever had just happened, Jacob had a distinct feeling that he was not out of danger.

He looked around to get his bearings and saw that he was in an apple orchard. Beautiful plump red apples were hanging from the trees, ready to be picked.

He walked farther into the orchard and saw some shrubby trees with skinny trunks and big leaves, but he wasn't sure what kind they were. As he walked farther still, he saw a small hut with piles of small green pods outside and smoke coming out of its chimney, and he smelled an unmistakable aroma: coffee beans.

Jacob's mind raced. Where was he?

CHAPTER 31

Dexter landed on Planet Archimedes in a state of anxiety that was extreme even by his own elevated standards. He tried to calculate how long it had been since they had blasted off from Earth, but because he had been flying so much between planets and through space, it was tough to estimate just how much time had elapsed. He was sure it had been at least a couple of days, which was more than enough time for his parents to go mad with worry, police to be notified, search parties organized, news stations called, and mass hysteria spread around their state. He dearly hoped that when he saw his parents in the Looking Glass, they wouldn't appear too worried.

"Lucy, what do you think I'm going to see?"

"I don't know," she said. "But you'd better make it snappy."

Dexter left the spaceship and walked toward the Looking Glass. The façade of the building was itself a giant mirror, with an ornate wooden frame around the edges and reflective glass covering all four sides. As he walked toward it Dexter could see himself approaching. He did not look at all like the confident kid he had resolved to be just a short while ago. The Era of Dexter was not off to a promising start, what with crying in front of a construction worker and not being able to find a way home. But he puffed up his chest, gave himself a bounce in his step, and told himself that whatever he was going to see in the Looking Glass, well, he could handle it.

He walked through the front door and into the foyer, which was entirely covered in mirrors. He stared at the floor, which reflected the ceiling, which reflected the walls, and he had to focus to stand upright because the effect was so disorienting. He wasn't sure which way to walk.

"Appellation?" asked a scientist sitting at a mirrored desk. Even her lab coat was made of reflective material. She had a deep, dry voice, and a slight accent that made her sound as if she would have felt quite at home in an old vampire movie.

"Huh?"

"Name, young man. What is your name?"

"Dexter Goldstein."

"And whom do you want to see?"

"My parents."

"I see." She typed Dexter's name into the desk and nodded. "Right this way."

Dexter followed the scientist into a cavernous room. He stared up at the mirrored ceiling, which was incredibly far away, and he looked very tiny, just a speck in a giant space. The scientist talked as they made their way toward the middle of the room.

"The Looking Glass will allow you to see anyone in the universe. All you have to do is think of a person, and through brain imaging and some patent-pending technological innovations the Looking Glass will show you these individuals. Space and time are not impediments. You may see them, but you will not be able to communicate with them. You must take care with the results, and do not use this device for any purpose other than research. We must adhere to the strongest ethics. No mucking about." She turned around and stared down at Dexter. "Do you understand?"

"I think so."

"Do you think so or do you know so?"

"Um . . ."

"Answer the question."

"Yes," Dexter said quietly. "I understand."

The scientist gave just the slightest upturn of the corners of her mouth, and she bowed. "Good. Right this way."

Dexter and the scientist approached a large mirror in the center of the room that had swirling gold edges and hovered in place. Even though Dexter had seen almost nothing but mirrors ever since he had entered the building, this one seemed different from the rest, even aside from the fact that it was hovering as if it were exempt from the laws of gravity. It had an almost otherworldly shimmer and a presence of its own, like a living thing.

"Now, Mr. Goldstein," the scientist said. "Whom do you want to see?"

"I already told—" he said.

"Don't tell me. Just think about them and you will see them."

Dexter thought quickly about Jacob and Sarah and Mick, but he knew there were more important things that he needed to know first. He had to make sure everyone was still alive on Earth.

Dexter took a deep breath and stared at the mirror.

He thought about his parents and concentrated on a mental image of their faces. Even though he had just heard the rules of the Looking Glass, he held out hope that they would somehow know that he was watching and that he was alive and that he needed their help. He wanted some sign or miracle that they could help him find his way home.

He noticed the light bending on the Looking Glass, and had the sudden sense that he could see all the way through it and that it was opening up a world in front of him.

The light rearranged itself, and Dexter saw his mother. His initial elation at seeing her alive and realizing Earth still existed soon gave way to panic as he saw that she was lying in a hospital bed, looking deathly pale, with tubes emanating from her body and a steady, terrifying beep counting her heartbeat. Her black hair, normally pulled back into a crisp bun, was messy and disheveled. She

stirred softly, as if she was uncomfortable but didn't have the strength to move.

The door to the room opened and Dexter's father walked in, his face pale and concerned.

Dexter's mother slowly turned to face him. "Have they found Dexy?"

His father looked away but didn't answer.

His mother stared back at the ceiling and took a

deep breath. After a moment a tear slid down her cheek.

"No!" Dexter shouted. "Mom, no! I'm okay!"

The image grew blurry, and then Dexter saw himself in the Looking Glass, looking hysterical and terrified.

"No!" he shouted again, his voice echoing across the distant walls. He turned to the scientist, who was standing serenely with her hands clasped. It was worse than he could have imagined. Not only was his mom in the hospital, but they were worried about him. It dawned on him that the stress of his disappearance must have made her sick. He could have been responsible for everything. "I have to get back to Earth. How can I get back to Earth? Please! She looks sick! What if she's going to die?"

"Did you say Earth?"

"Yes! Please, the route is under construction and I have to get back. I have to, I have to!" Dexter's voice cracked and he searched the scientist's face for some signal that she would help him. "Please!"

"How old are you, young man?" the scientist asked.

"I'm . . . twelve and . . . What does that have to do with anything?"

"A twelve-year-old Earther," the scientist said, scratching her chin. "Very curious."

"Listen to me!"

The scientist stared off into the distance. "Why, what's that over there?"

Dexter turned and looked, but all he saw were distant mirrors. "What? Where?"

He felt a strong hand on his shoulder and a cloth over his nose that smelled like cough medicine. He tried to scream, but his voice wouldn't come. He felt suddenly numb and weak.

And then everything went black.

CHAPTER 32

Sarah Daisy stared at herself in the full-length mirror in her suite on Planet Royale. She was wearing a long black dress that brought out her blond hair and blue eyes. Her ears felt heavy from long jeweled earrings, and she wore a silver necklace with a large green gemstone. She had never, ever dressed up so fancily before, even for her biggest piano recitals. Part of her wanted to tear it all off and find the nearest pair of jeans, but another part of her actually kind of enjoyed the way the dress moved in the mirror.

She had waited all day for the gala, desperately searching for something to do. First she had walked down to the lagoon to try to talk to the pink dolphin, but she soon learned that dolphins weren't particularly interesting conversationalists. She searched the palace grounds for an escape route, finding all sorts of storerooms filled with pillows and chandeliers and bathrobes and slippers, but she didn't find any possible hint of a way off the planet. She tried to get a suntan but didn't last five minutes lying still, and even took Sven up on his offer to book an appointment with the royal masseuse, an ancient woman with white hair and hands of steel. Sarah made sure that the appointment involved rigorous tapping and strange contortions because at least that was somewhat entertaining. She found the cook and offered to help him with the next meal, but he was too distracted to speak to her. She even caught a glimpse of the king, a tall man with white hair, walking around the gardens with his hands clasped in contemplation, but she ducked and ran away, too scared to talk to him.

After pretending a pillow was a soccer ball and kicking it around her suite, and tapping out a sonata silently on the desk, Sarah finally yelled, "Get me out of here!" and after no one came to rescue her, she began dressing for the gala, where at least she might be able to use some of the steps she learned in ballet.

As she was admiring her dress in the mirror, she heard a proper voice say, "Mistress Daisy?"

She looked around and up at the ceiling and she grinned. "Praiseworthy?!"

"Oh, great goose's gold, it's so good to hear your voice! The palace's computer allowed me on his circuits so that I could tell you that I'm sure you look simply beautiful and dazzling, and you will be the envy of tonight's gala."

Sarah's eyebrows went up in happiness and she thought she might cry. "Praiseworthy, that's so nice! I'm so glad you're here. I've missed you so much."

Suddenly a loud alarm went off and lights began flashing. Sarah looked around in confusion.

"Mistress Daisy," Praiseworthy whispered urgently. "You must save me! The palace mechanics are going to paint me pink and turn me back into a princess party cruiser. Oh, the humanity! I simply can't bear it. I've created a diversion. Run! Run! Please help me! I can only keep the palace's computer at bay for so long!"

"Where are you? I've been looking all over for you!"

"The spaceport is at the end of the hall to your right! I've unlocked the door for you. Please hurry!"

Sarah ran out into the hall and closed the door behind her. She peered down the long hallway of the palace and began walking briskly. Red lights were flashing and the alarm was sounding throughout the palace. She saw a servant at the other end of the hall waving his arms at her. "Miss Daisy, you must move outside, the alarms . . ."

Sarah smiled and pointed down the hall. "I'm just . . . um . . . going . . . and . . . um . . . yeah." She grimaced at her poor performance and hoped the servant wouldn't follow her.

She kept on walking toward the spaceport and breathed a sigh of relief when she entered and saw Praiseworthy, still painted a sloppy black. "You came!" he shouted. "Oh, Mistress Daisy, this is such a happy day."

"Let's get out of here, Praiseworthy!"

"How I hoped you would say that! Yee-haw!"

Sarah wanted to hug him even though he was a huge spaceship. But a figure stepped out of the shadows.

"I thought I'd find you here," Mick Cracken said with one of his insufferable grins. He was wearing a tuxedo with shimmering fabric, and his hair was actually arranged properly rather than its typical mess of tangles. Sarah had to admit that he had cleaned up into something approaching handsome, even if his cocky grin ruined the effect.

"What do *you* want?" Sarah said with her hands on her hips.

Mick's mischievous grin morphed into an innocent smile. The change in expression was a Mick Cracken specialty. "You look lovely. Black is the perfect color on you. You're a vision."

Sarah rolled her eyes.

"I came to apologize," he said. "I'm sorry I lied to you. I said some things I shouldn't have. And I hope you'll forgive me. I know I doubted that you like me."

"I don't like you," she said.

Mick smiled again and stepped slowly toward her. "Exactly. It shows you like me for who I am. Or rather dislike me for who I am. You're not caught up in . . ." Mick waved his hand. "All this. So many people are."

Up close Mick's freckles weren't quite as ugly as she had thought they were and his eyes were very blue, although she certainly didn't choose her friends based on their eye color. She appreciated that he knew he had been wrong and decided to apologize to her. Perhaps he was merely partially rotten instead of completely rotten.

"I'm sorry too," she said. "For being rude to you sometimes. Even though you mostly deserved it."

"An apology from Sarah Daisy." Mick laughed. "I never thought I'd see the day."

"Enjoy it while you can, bucko," Sarah said sternly, although she let a smile creep through. She even chose to overlook that he had just violated the rules by saying her full name.

She stepped forward and hugged Mick, who tensed

with surprise and then put his arms around her. He was actually a decent person for a boy.

But he was no Jacob Wonderbar.

She pulled back and looked him in the eyes. "I'm leaving, Mick."

"Why?"

Her face glowed and she felt a sudden rush of excitement. She couldn't wait to get off the royal planet and hoped she'd never be forced to relax again. And this time she really would be the one in charge.

"I have to go save Jacob Wonderbar."

She ran aboard Praiseworthy and left Mick behind.

CHAPTER 33

Jacob stepped slowly to the edge of the forest of apple and coffee trees. He saw a clearing up ahead and heard some faint noises and music. He hid behind a tree and carefully peered around, fearful of what he might find.

In the middle of the clearing was a large swimming pool surrounded by adults wearing old one-piece bathing suits. Many of them were reading magazines and drinking coffee, and they looked as if they had not been out in the sun in years. Several adults were sitting at a table nearby playing Scrabble and some were reading thousand-page books. Classical music was blasting from a nearby stereo.

Jacob snuck closer to a table and heard one of the adults say, "And I told our union rep that we needed to have a spring week like they have in the next county over, but with all the cutbacks, they can't even get my health insurance straightened out, and I don't even know what in the world I'm going to do when the summer comes."

The other adults clucked in sympathy. "Sounds like Ms. Plummer is going to have a bummer of a summer," someone said. The other adults tittered.

He racked his brain trying to figure out who these people were. They were dressed somewhat similarly as the substitutes, and yet they were clearly something different.

"Young man," Jacob heard a woman say.

Jacob turned around and his eyes nearly popped out of his head. It wasn't possible. The woman in front of him was someone he knew, but how in the heck could he actually find someone he knew in outer space? He wiped his eyes and looked again. No mistake. He was face-to-face with his teacher. From Earth. "Miss Banks?! It's . . . you?"

"Jacob? What in the world are you doing here?"

"What are you doing here?" Jacob shouted.

"That's what I said!"

Jacob reached out and grabbed a tree to steady himself. "I don't believe this."

"Jacob, how did you get here? Take your time. Do you need an apple?"

Jacob took deep breaths. Miss Banks? On Planet Paisley? He tried to make sense of it all. He looked over and there she was, short blond hair, thin glasses, and slightly twitchy hands. It was really her. But something was very different and very, very wrong. He tried to figure out what was strange about her, and then it hit him.

"Miss Banks, you're wearing jeans!"

Miss Banks looked down and laughed. "When I'm not at school, Jacob, yes, sometimes I wear jeans."

"I didn't think teachers were allowed to wear jeans."

"Believe it or not, it's perfectly legal."

Jacob wasn't so sure that it should be. But he looked up at her and could only think of one thing to say. "What are you doing here?"

"Where do you think teachers go when you have substitutes? Oh, Jacob, this place is heavenly. They have all the fresh coffee you could ever want, we sit around discussing current events for hours, we give each other brain teasers . . ." Miss Banks closed her eyes and sighed. "It's magical."

Jacob looked over at the adults sitting near the pool. "They're all teachers?"

"You should have heard the wonderful haiku that Mr. Harrison came up with. It was such a hoot, and—"

"Are all of my substitutes from this planet?"

"Of course! The Astrals were getting so scared of Earth, they wanted to try to rehabilitate Earth children, and with all the budget cuts, the free substitutes came in quite handy. But usually the subs are just so bewildered they . . ." Something occurred to Miss Banks and she looked back down at Jacob. "What happened to Mrs. Pinkerton? Don't tell me that you terrorized her too. Do you know how hard it was to get someone from this planet to take over my class?"

Jacob laughed nervously.

"You're notorious! I had to promise Mrs. Pinkerton a year's worth of number two pencils just to get her to even consider it."

"How many Astrals are there on Earth?"

"I don't know about that. Only the king knows for sure. But let me tell you, once you know there are Astrals on Earth, pretty soon everyone starts looking like a space human."

"The king? What . . ."

Another adult materialized nearby. She handed a pink note to Miss Banks. "From the principal's office," she said.

Miss Banks peered through her glasses to read the note, then turned her head to Jacob with alarm.

"Jacob, is this true?!"

Jacob wondered what the note said and realized there

were any number of messages it could have contained that would have been cause for a great deal of alarm. Jacob decided to tread cautiously. "Is what true?"

"You evaded an angry band of substitute teachers?"

Jacob felt a rush of pride, but he tried not to show it. "They almost lassoed me with earphones, but I got away."

Miss Banks laughed in that high, chipper way that he sometimes heard in class. She looked around and then leaned forward and whispered, "The subs *are* kind of strange, aren't they?"

Jacob looked over at a group of teachers playing badminton and thought that perhaps Miss Banks shouldn't be the one calling people strange.

"How did you get here?" Miss Banks asked again.

Jacob scratched his head. "Well, I got arrested on a planet full of scientists and they ditched me here. Oh. And I kind of broke the universe."

Miss Banks's eyes went wide. "That was you? Do you know I can't get back to Earth because of that mess?"

"Earth's okay?!"

"Of course it is! Why wouldn't it be?"

Jacob closed his eyes and thanked the stars. He took a deep breath and steadied his knees.

"Good thing I like it here." Miss Banks laughed

again. "Oh, Jacob Wonderbar. You know what? Of all the kids I've had over the years, I can't say I'm terribly surprised that it was you who found a way to outer space. You're a pretty special kid."

"Thanks," Jacob mumbled, embarrassed at the compliment.

Miss Banks looked at him with that serious and earnest expression teachers adopted whenever they were about to impart a piece of wisdom. "Jacob, I know you've had some real challenges the last couple of years. And I'm very, very sorry about that. You're a special kid, and . . . well, I've already said too much, haven't I?"

Jacob blushed when he realized that Miss Banks probably knew everything about him, including his father leaving home, his mom's frustration with his problems at school, and possibly his blood type and dental records. But Miss Banks was different from the other teachers. She looked at him through those glasses and it was like she saw past what was actually happening in the moment and could see what was *really* happening.

Jacob cleared his throat and said, "I'm sorry I let the air out of your bike tires."

Miss Banks smiled. "It turned out to be a nice walk home."

She hadn't written him off like nearly everyone else

at school. She thought there was more to him. She thought he showed promise.

"Time to run, Jacob," Miss Banks said. "The note said you're wanted in the principal's office. Trust me, you don't want to go to the principal's office. You'd probably be assigned so much detention, you'd never be able to leave this planet. What do you say we let bygones be bygones and you consider this a head start back to the spaceport?"

Jacob hugged Miss Banks, who patted him on the back in a motherly way. "Now, now," she said. "Let's not get emotional."

"Thank you, Miss Banks," Jacob said. "You're the best teacher ever."

"Well," she said, her eyes twinkling, "that's what every teacher wants to hear their kids say someday." She winked at him. "And Planet Paisley is our secret."

Jacob nodded and ran toward Substitute City, but he stopped and turned back. "How am I going to get home?" he asked.

Miss Banks smiled. "I think you'll find a way."

CHAPTER 34

When Dexter woke up, his head felt as if it weighed a thousand pounds. He thought back to what had happened and remembered seeing his parents in the Looking Glass and the scary scientist and the smell of cough syrup and the memory hit him hard . . . Had he been drugged? Was he kidnapped?

When he finally had the power to open his eyes, he stared upward at a distant black ceiling. He gathered his strength, sat up slowly, and looked around at his surroundings. He was in what looked like a small room with smooth gray walls on three sides, which opened up to a long corridor. The walls didn't extend to the ceiling, but they were too tall for him to see over.

"Hello?"

He didn't hear a response.

Dexter stood up and started walking slowly down the hallway. He reached the end, and to the right it opened up to . . . another hallway. He walked down that one until it ended and he had a choice about whether to go left or right. He chose right and walked until he had to turn right again and reached a dead end.

Dexter felt his chest tighten when he realized what was happening. He was in a maze.

He remembered the last time he was in a human maze, which was during Jacob Wonderbar's eighth birthday party. Dexter had felt so nervous about being lost and trapped with no escape that he began envisioning scenarios where he would never find his way out and the staff wouldn't be able to find him because they too would get lost, and he had eventually concluded that he was going to end up starving to death at a dead end. Dexter grew so panicked that he charged straight through an emergency exit, which set off all sorts of alarms, enraged a pimply teenaged maze staff member, and very quickly ended what he hoped would be his last maze adventure.

Jacob's mom had taken pity on him and explained in a very calm and rational fashion that he didn't have to be scared of mazes because there was a very simple way to escape them that didn't involve panic attacks and emergency exits.

Dexter took a deep breath. Now he just needed to remember what that method was.

Dexter turned back around and reached the previous crossroads. This time he went left. He reached out and touched the wall and suddenly he remembered. All he had to do was keep touching the wall with one hand and he would find a way out. As long as he never let go and kept walking forward and always turned left, he would never double back and waste time. It worked on most mazes, and he hoped this was one of them.

Dexter began running through the maze with his

left hand on the wall. Dead ends didn't faze him. Neither did crossroads. He kept choosing left, and when he hit a dead end he just kept his hand on the wall and kept right on running.

Finally he saw something different up ahead. It was huge and sparkly and looked like . . . a really big diamond. It was the Dragon's Eye, the very thing that had caused them to fight and split up. He realized that Jacob and Sarah must not have been able to steal it after all. Dexter wondered if it could grant wishes and get him out of a maze and back to Planet Earth.

Dexter stepped forward carefully. He noticed a sign on the front, and walked toward it until he could read it.

It said: "Do you want to steal this?"

There were buttons for "yes" and "no."

Dexter wondered if it was a trick question, but he had a feeling he needed to answer correctly. He thought about running up and making a wish for a million wishes and then wishing himself back to Earth.

But he looked again at the sign. It said "steal," and Dexter wondered if it was a trap all over again. The Dragon's Eye had separated his friends and distracted them all from finding a way home. They had fought over it, and it was the final straw that separated him from Jacob and Sarah. Trick question or not, Dexter knew exactly how he should answer.

He punched the "no" button, and suddenly all of the walls of the maze rose up to the sky. He was in a huge laboratory.

A scientist with a red bow tie came bounding over to shake Dexter's hand. "Thank you for your participation in our experiment, young man! Splendid! You have no idea how difficult it is to find twelve-year-old Earthers on our planet." He handed Dexter a piece of paper. "Here is a coupon for a free microscope to compensate you for your time."

Dexter stared at the coupon. "I . . . What was this about? Why did you drug me?"

The scientist was bursting with pride. "We had a trial by scientific method and developed a theory that a twelve-year-old Earther was guilty of the attempted theft of our priceless carbon allotrope in order to start a war. However, we are scientists and mustn't jump to conclusions until all experiments are independently verified, but we've just had the hardest time—"

"You're talking about a twelve-year-old who stole a diamond?"

"Why, yes. In layman's terms."

Dexter knew of only two twelve-year-old Earth humans who could have possibly gotten caught trying to steal the Dragon's Eye, and Sarah Daisy never got into trouble. "Was it Jacob Wonderbar?! Where is he?"

The scientist scratched his chin. "No, I seem to recall that this individual was either Mick Cracken disguised as an Earther or a girl disguised as a boy. Possibly both. He was sent to Planet Paisley to be rehabilitated. We can't very well have suspected carbon allotrope thieves running around our planet, now can we?"

Someone named a planet after paisley? But Dexter shook the question out of his head. He had more important considerations.

"Listen," Dexter said. "I have to get back to Earth. My mother is sick! Please help me!"

"Oh dear," the scientist said. "That is quite a complex scenario. If I'm not mistaken, the main route to Earth was blocked recently by a colossal space explosion."

"I know it is! I helped cause that mess!"

The scientist frowned. "Why would you do that?"

"It was an accident!" Dexter felt like he might cry out of frustration. "Listen to me!" he yelled with as much force as he had ever used in his life.

The room silenced and everyone looked at Dexter.

"My parents are worried and my mom is sick. I have to find a way back to Earth. Please help me go home."

The scientist glanced at his colleagues and then back

to Dexter. "Young man, under the circumstances, I believe there is only one person in the universe who can help you."

Dexter felt a glimmer of hope. "Who? Who can help me?"

"The king."

"The king of what?"

"The king of everything."

CHAPTER 35

When Sarah blasted off from the palace on Planet Royale, she was glad to be leaving. Planet Royale was designed for pure relaxation, and Sarah Daisy now knew she found relaxation terrifically boring.

"Where shall I set my course, Mistress Daisy?" Praiseworthy asked.

Sarah wondered how she would find Jacob and Dexter. A few days had gone by and they could be anywhere. The only thing she could think to do was to head back to the place where she had last seen them and start looking for clues.

"Planet Archimedes," she said.

Sarah leaned back in the captain's chair and settled

in for the journey. She could squeeze in a bit more shut-eye and chat with Praiseworthy while she was awake to keep herself entertained, and be ready to tackle any obstacle that stood in her way when she finally found Jacob and Dexter.

Then she heard a familiar voice in the cockpit.

"Ugh. Praiseworthy, you've *got* to be kidding me. Don't tell me they only stocked two days worth of chocolate."

Sarah felt her stomach drop. Mistress Silver Spoon.

"Oh dear me, Princess Catalina," Praiseworthy said. "It's all my fault. I asked the staff to supply a variety of candy products so that there would be an assortment of anything you could possibly desire on the voyage, but I fear this reduced the amount of chocolate in proportion to the entire dessert supply. I do hope you can find it within your grace to forgive me."

Mistress Silver Spoon plopped herself next to Sarah in the first mate's chair and kicked up her feet on the console. She was dressed casually in pants and a long T-shirt, although her ears were studded with some of the biggest jeweled earrings Sarah had ever seen. She leaned over and air-kissed a stunned Sarah on both cheeks.

"Ciao, darling." Princess Catalina popped a piece of chocolate into her mouth.

"What are you doing here?!" Sarah shrieked.

"This *is* my ship, you know," she said with a full mouth.

Sarah clenched her fists. The princess had actually snuck on board?! It was an outrage. She immediately began casting about for ways of getting rid of her, but she couldn't very well risk going back to Planet Royale to dump Mistress Silver Spoon on her silly throne. Surely the royal fleet wouldn't have taken kindly to an unauthorized departure, and she might even have to answer to the king. Sarah looked over at the princess and wondered why on Planet Royale she could have possibly wanted to stow away on her trip.

"Ugh," Princess Catalina said, rolling her eyes. "Don't look so surprised, Earth girl. It's not an attractive look on you. You know, my brother isn't the only one who likes to have fun around here."

Sarah had a sudden fantasy of jettisoning the princess onto a remote planet, but she didn't suppose Mistress Silver Spoon could be tricked on her own ship.

Princess Catalina swallowed her chocolate and clapped gleefully. "So! Where are we going?"

Sarah clenched her jaw and muttered, "Planet Archimedes."

"You're taking me to nerd paradise?!" Princess Catalina slumped her head back and sprawled her arms

225

like she was in agony. "Ugh. I should have known. Are you going to quiz me on word problems along the way? You'll probably spend the whole time working on your homework. Nightmare city! Couldn't we at least go to Planet Galleria and shop until we collapse? Oh! Better yet, let's go to Planet Girlfriend. It's where all the stylists live, and they're a little sassy, but we could work on that hair of yours."

Sarah felt her cheeks getting hot. "We have to go there to find my friends Jacob and Dexter."

Princess Catalina shot up in her seat. "Boys? Really? Are they cute?"

Sarah had a sudden vision of Jacob Wonderbar falling head over heels for the princess. "No," she lied. "They're not cute."

Princess Catalina looked Sarah over. "I probably shouldn't have gotten my hopes up."

"What's that supposed to mean?!"

Princess Catalina smiled and raised her eyebrows up and down quickly. "So what do you say? Are we going to have all kinds of adventures? Are we going to go rescue the boys and make them wait on us hand and foot? What do you say, Earth girl?"

There was nothing in the universe that Sarah would rather have done less than cavort around with Princess Catalina. It was tremendously taxing on her ability to avoid anger and violence. But when she considered the alternatives, she didn't see much of a choice. As long as she wanted to keep heading toward Planet Archimedes and hold out hope of finding Jacob and Dexter, she figured she would have to make the best of it.

"Fine," Sarah said through her teeth.

Princess Catalina flashed Sarah a smile that reeked of victory and satisfaction. A Crackenarium family specialty, apparently. Sarah thought she might be sick.

Praiseworthy whooped with joy. "Giant green gum-drops, I just knew you would be friends!"

CHAPTER 36

Jacob crept down an eerily silent street in Substitute City. He had managed to avoid detection, but he knew that gangly substitute teacher evildoers could be lurking around every corner. He wasn't far from the city's spaceport, but he wasn't sure how long he would be able to escape their clutches.

He was still stunned that he had run into Miss Banks. He had no idea how she would get back to Earth herself now that there was a giant streak across the sky that just happened to be blocking the most expedient route back to their planet. But mostly he was shocked by the discovery that there was a whole universe that teachers had hidden from him and who knows how many other Astrals cavorting around Earth. All those UFO sightings now made a great deal more sense.

Jacob saw a group of menacing subs crossing the street up ahead. They hadn't seen him, but just to be safe, he ducked into a store and quickly closed the door.

He looked around at a dusty room filled with antiques and old school supplies. The wall was covered by old maps that showed what were surely out-of-date countries and borders. He saw a dunce cap, old typewriters, and a paddle.

A wizened old man sat behind the counter. Jacob froze.

"Are you a substitute teacher?" Jacob asked, ready to run.

"Used to be a janitor," the man said. "Now I'm a collector. This here is a pawnshop slash antique store. I collected from schools on planets all around the galaxy. Most of this stuff people don't want anymore. I think it's a crying shame."

Jacob relaxed and ran his finger over an old metal desk that opened up with compartments for pencils and rulers. He saw inkwells and fountain pens, old wooden pointers, jars full of marbles, and coffee mugs of every shape, design, and age. He spotted an old movie projector and touched the metal spool.

"You have old movies?"

The old man smiled, walked over, and switched it on. The sound warbled and the black-and-white picture flickered to life, skipping and scratching. A stern voice warned children about the dangers of communism and the possibility of a nuclear explosion and mushroom clouds. They showed children dropping to the ground and hiding underneath their desks. There was a flash of light, but the kids were safe afterward, and the stern voice talked about freedom and democracy.

"Wow," Jacob said. "Would a desk really protect you from a nuclear explosion? That's kind of amazing."

"Nope," the old man said. "That was a bunch of hooey. Thought you'd enjoy seeing it, though."

The old man switched off the projector and Jacob walked over to look at the items in the glass case at the front of the store.

The old man rifled through some reels. "I think I have one about the origins of Astrals, do you want to watch that?"

Jacob didn't even hear him. He was staring at a pipe in the glass case. It was made out of old wood that was polished into a fine shine, and it had a charming, jaunty curve, with a streaked base that swooped up to a small black tip. There was a pewter stripe in the middle that held the pieces together.

He was sure that he had seen it before.

"Can I please see that pipe?" he asked quietly.

The old man wordlessly opened the case, took out

the pipe, and placed it gently on the glass in front of Jacob. His hands shook when he carefully picked it up, turned it over, and looked at the base.

Jacob couldn't believe it. Of all the things to see in outer space. He just couldn't make sense of it.

"It's my dad's," he finally managed to say.

He showed the man the base of the pewter, where the name Wonderbar was inscribed.

It was the pipe Jacob's dad had used when he dressed up as Sherlock Holmes on his birthdays. He used to fill the pipe with bubbles and would adopt a serious expression, asking Jacob ridiculous questions and blowing into the pipe as he waited for Jacob to reply. Jacob could hardly think straight, his dad looked so hilarious,

and he could still hear the way he said, "But what do you think it *means,* Dr. Watson?" in a British accent.

The pipe had once belonged to his grandfather, an imposing German man who had died before Jacob was born. He put it up to his nose, and it still smelled faintly of bubbles and old tobacco.

"Where did you get this?" Jacob finally said. "Did it come from Earth?"

The old man scratched his chin. "No son, it did not come from Earth. Can't say I remember which planet it came from, though. I've been to so many. Definitely did not find it on Earth, I can say that."

"How many planets are there?" Jacob asked.

The man chuckled. "More than you can even imagine."

Jacob knew how much his dad loved the pipe. He never would have parted with it unless he was either in trouble or . . . gone. Jacob swallowed nervously at that thought, which had never occurred to him. But a part of him just knew his dad wasn't dead. He couldn't be.

"Do all the adults on Earth know about space?"

The man scratched his cheek. "Only the lucky ones."

"My dad's in outer space," he said quietly.

Then he turned around and looked at the old man. "Can I have this?"

The old man frowned. "Don't think I should be handing out pipes to young men."

"Please? It's been in my family for generations. Look at the inscription. My name is Jacob Wonderbar."

The old man waved his hand and looked away like he didn't want to think about it anymore. "Just don't tell anyone."

It explained so much. Maybe his dad hadn't moved away after all. All these years he could have been bouncing around space, just like Jacob, trying to find his way home. He could have been stopped from returning even if he wanted to come back. He could have been lost in the craziness of outer space. And now with the space kapow, there was no way for him to get to Earth. He would be blocked from returning, just like Jacob.

Jacob clutched the pipe to his chest and wondered if he could actually find his dad.

CHAPTER 37

Sarah had reached a tentative truce with Princess Catalina by the time they arrived at Planet Archimedes. She was surprised that the princess hadn't insisted on taking command of the ship with that bossy way of hers, and instead she just seemed thrilled to be along for the ride. She asked Sarah all about her life on Earth, and they spent plenty of time discussing the topic of Earth boys.

They even sat down for some incredibly delicious tea in the room where Mick had defaced Princess Catalina's portrait.

"Doesn't that bother you?" Sarah asked.

Princess Catalina looked up at the portrait and laughed. "What, that? You have to admit it's kind of funny. Don't worry your little head, I'll get him back."

Sarah couldn't imagine what she would have done to her little sister if she had defaced one of her pictures, but it probably would have involved violent actions that would be considered felonies in most states. She marveled at the way Princess Catalina just let it slide off her back like it didn't mean anything.

"I have a strange question I've been dying to ask," Sarah said. "Do all animals in outer space talk? I think I heard a mouse try to boss me around and I tried talking to the little pink dolphin . . ."

"Oh, Mortimer. He's such a cutie-patootie," she laughed. "No, silly, not *all* the animals. The scientists just enhanced some of the animals so the cute ones can talk. No one wants to know what a tarantula has to say."

"The scientists? The ones from Planet Archimedes?"

"Duh."

"You can't imagine the agony it causes me to interrupt this bonding session," Praiseworthy interjected, "but we've arrived in the orbit of Planet Archimedes. Do continue your conversation on our arrival, and please know how happy it makes me that you two are such good friends."

Sarah looked over quickly at Catalina, expecting

her to roll her eyes at the suggestion that they were friends, but instead the princess gave her a sparkling, happy smile. Sarah almost choked on her tea. Did she think they were actually friends?

"So?" Princess Catalina said. "Where do you suppose we'll find your friends on Planet Dork?"

Sarah had an idea. "Praiseworthy, can you run a search for the spaceship Lucy on this planet?"

"Mistress Daisy, it would give me great pleasure to do so. I was never able to finish telling her about my rocket boosters and would be ever so happy to reacquaint with her."

Sarah moved to the cockpit and watched as Praiseworthy swooped down to the planet and landed near a building that looked like a giant mirror.

They stepped outside and walked over to Lucy. It gave Sarah a thrill to see the old metal pipes and copper plating, and she thought about when she had seen Lucy for the first time in the moonlit forest. It had seemed so incredible then. She had almost gotten used to flying around space. Sarah peeked inside the hold and yelled, "Jake? Dexter?"

That was when she heard a scream. It was coming from outside.

Sarah jumped out of Lucy's hold and looked over at the front of the mirrored building. She saw Dexter, running away as fast as he could and letting out a long, loud yell all the way.

"Dexter!" Sarah shouted.

Dexter kept on running until he reached Sarah, and stopped in front of her, panting.

"It's . . . I'm . . . My parents . . . King . . . Kidnapped . . ."

Sarah stepped over and patted him on the back. "Take your time, Dexter."

He leaned over and put his hands on his knees. "Hyp . . . hyper . . . hyperventilation."

Princess Catalina clapped her hands. "I'm having so much fun!"

Dexter finally caught his breath, stood up, and said, "It's my parents, they're . . . We have to . . ." He looked at Sarah, confused. "Why are you all dressed up?"

Sarah looked down at her dress. She had almost forgotten that she was still wearing the black ball gown and the jewelry from the gala that she never attended. Her face turned red. She snapped, "Would you like to try that again, Dexter Goldstein?"

Dexter sensed that he was suddenly on thin ice and he searched for the right thing to say. "Um . . . Where did you get the dress? Is it a designer I should know about or something?"

"Ugh!" Sarah said. "You are impossible."

Princess Catalina stepped around her and offered her hand to Dexter, fingers down, waiting for him to kiss it. Dexter stared at her hand for a moment in confusion and reached out and shook it quickly.

"I'm Princess Catalina Penelope Cassandra Crackenarium. You can call me Cat."

Sarah's anger reached another decibel. Dexter got to call her "Cat" but she insisted that Sarah call her "Princess Catalina"?

"I'm Dexter." Dexter stared at the princess, then at Sarah. "Do I need to bow or something?"

Catalina laughed and batted her eyes. "Such a funny boy."

Dexter looked up quickly. "Wait. If you're the princess, that means you might know the king! The king of everything!"

Catalina laughed again. "And he's smart too. Of course, Dex. The king is my daddy, silly!"

That was the last straw. Sarah was ready to step in. Calling him "Dex" was just one outrage too many. She was about to speak up, but Dexter grabbed Sarah by the arm as if he had gone mad. "Sarah! The scientists told me that seeing the king is the only way we can get home. He can help us get back to Earth!"

Sarah turned on Princess Catalina. "Is this true?"

Princess Catalina rolled her eyes. "Darling, he is the *king* after all."

"Why didn't you tell me?!"

"Sarah, I saw my parents," Dexter said. "My mom is in trouble."

"Your mom?" Princess Catalina gasped. "What happened?"

"My mom is sick!" Dexter said. He turned around and pointed at the mirrored building. "They have a mirror where you can see what's happening to anyone in the universe. I saw my mom. She was in the hospital. They're so worried, and . . ." Dexter trailed off. "I think she might be dying."

Sarah was about to say something when Princess Catalina stepped forward and hugged Dexter. Sarah saw that she had tears in her eyes and she held him tightly. "You poor thing," she said. She rocked Dexter back and forth. "I know just how you feel. My mom had cancer."

Sarah stood in anguish, thinking that she should have been the one to hug Dexter first. She did the best thing that she could do, which was to step over and rub his back softly. "I'm so sorry, Dexter."

Catalina broke the hug, and Dexter sniffed and said, "Thanks." He looked at Sarah when he said it.

"We'll get home soon," Sarah said. "We really will. We just have to find Jacob. Is he here? Do you know where he is?"

Dexter nodded. "The scientists said he's on something called Planet Paisley."

Princess Catalina threw up her hands. "You're kidding me. Planet Paisley?! You people sure pick the worst planets to have your adventures."

CHAPTER 38

Lucy opted out of the trip to Planet Paisley due to a high likelihood of boredom, and so the children bounded onto Praiseworthy and blasted off. Dexter told Sarah what had happened ever since they'd been separated, from getting jettisoned by Mick to being stuck on a little planet called Numonia, eating space dust to fighting with Jacob, the trip to the edge of the space kapow and back, seeing his parents in a mirror, and somehow ending up drugged and placed in a human maze.

Sarah could barely pay attention because her heart was racing so quickly. All she could think about was Jacob Wonderbar.

Mostly she wondered if he hated her. Whenever she

thought about the look of betrayal on his face when she escaped the museum with Mick, she wanted to punch a wall out of frustration. She hoped he would understand how sorry she was. She had blown it, and she knew it.

Sarah was quiet when she arrived at the spaceport with Catalina and Dexter, who were chatting away about space and everything they were seeing along the way. Sarah might have thought that Catalina was doing a good job of distracting Dexter from how scared he was about his mom, but she wasn't sure that shifty girl ever had good intentions.

When they arrived on Planet Paisley, they stepped out onto the street and looked at the pedestrians streaming by. Sarah hadn't ever seen such an intense concentration of questionable fashion choices.

"Who are these people?" Dexter whispered in awe.

"They're substitute teachers," Catalina said quietly. "And we really shouldn't be here."

"Substitute teachers?!" Dexter whispered. "On another planet?" He ran through a mental inventory of his Jacob Wonderbar–inspired antics with subs over the years. "This is not good."

They heard a commotion nearby and saw a crowd of substitutes shouting and raising their fists. The children looked at one another and then ran over.

"Suspend him!" someone shouted.

"Give him ten demerits!"

"Take away his extracurricular activities!"

"Call his parents and suggest he's not reaching his full potential!"

Though they weren't tall enough to see over the shoulders of the subs, Sarah caught a glimpse of Jacob Wonderbar through the shifting commotion. He was in trouble and looked frightened.

"Jake!" she shrieked.

The subs turned around and looked at her, and Sarah slowly began backing up as a group of them crept toward her.

"Do you have a hall pass?" one of the subs asked menacingly.

"Young lady, we will not stand for this kind of disruption," another said.

Sarah raised her hands in innocence. "Now . . . Let's be reasonable! Can't I just write you a paper on the Berlin Airlift?"

Jacob watched the events unfold in a daze. His friends had come back for him? Sarah was wearing a dress? He worried suddenly about Dexter, who was probably on a substitute teacher Most Wanted poster somewhere for being his number one accomplice during countless successful pranks.

That was when Jacob remembered the mortal weakness of every substitute teacher in the universe.

He pointed at Dexter. "That's the real Jacob Wonderbar!"

All of the subs stopped what they were doing and turned toward Dexter. They stared at him in confusion. A look of betrayal passed over Dexter's face and Jacob knew he was adding to the tally of all the times Jacob had tried to get him into trouble.

Jacob yelled, "I switched seats with Jacob at the beginning of class and ha-ha, we fooled you all!"

A young sub looked between Jacob and Dexter. He shook his head. "You're not fooling us this time."

"Take roll," Jacob said. He mentally crossed his fingers. He needed Dexter to set aside their fight and agree to one last prank. "I said take roll!"

"Jacob *Voonderbar*?" an elderly sub asked, looking down at a clipboard.

The subs looked back and forth between Jacob and Dexter.

Jacob held his breath.

"Present!" Dexter shouted.

The subs gasped. "It's him!" one of the subs shouted, pointing at Dexter. "It's Jacob Wonderbar, get him!"

Dexter turned and ran. All of the subs broke away

from Jacob and Sarah and chased after Dexter, but they were nowhere near fast enough.

Dexter raised a fist as he ran, and was engulfed by a sense of triumph that he hadn't felt in years. He had helped save Jacob Wonderbar.

"I pronounce this the Era of Dexter!" he yelled.

Soon Jacob and Sarah had caught up with Dexter and Catalina. They turned and looked at the subs trying in vain to chase them, and laughed hysterically all the way back to Praiseworthy.

CHAPTER 39

Aboard Praiseworthy, the children caught their breath, red-faced and gasping and laughing about their escape from the subs. As Jacob looked around the room, first at Dexter and Sarah, then at a fancy girl whom he had never seen before, various events began flashing through his mind. His fight with Dexter. Seeing Sarah with the Dragon's Eye and realizing she left him behind on Numonia. Sarah leaving again with Mick. His mood darkened and he reached down and felt the pipe in his pocket, a reminder of his unfinished business in outer space.

Before he could start to confront anyone, the fancy girl looked at Jacob, laughed merrily, and said, "Sarah Daisy, you rascal! You didn't tell me that I was going to meet my future husband on this trip!"

"Don't call me Sarah Daisy," Sarah said, glaring at Catalina. But rather than sounding tough, her voice was tentative. She looked at Jacob out of the corner of her eye.

The princess turned to Jacob with a winning smile. "I'm Princess Catalina. But you can call me your girl-friend." Catalina proffered her hand to Jacob, who smiled with embarrassment but kissed it anyway.

"You're a princess?" he asked.

Dexter cleared his throat with what sounded like annoyance and possibly jealousy. "Excuse me, may I have a word? Wonderbar, I don't know if we're still friends or what, but we have to get back to Earth as soon as possible."

Sarah stepped forward. "He's right, Jake. We have to—"

"We're in danger!" Praiseworthy shouted. "Jumping jellybeans, there is a ship in pursuit and it is very fast!"

The children scrambled into the cockpit.

"Where is it?" Dexter asked.

"There!" Jacob shouted. He spotted the ship on one of the monitors. It was a large spaceship shaped like a giant chalkboard eraser. It was bearing down on them quickly. He peered at the monitor.

"Monitor four, zoom in!" Jacob ordered.

The monitor refocused. He saw some determined

subs in the cockpit. Jacob grabbed on to the captain's chair. They weren't giving up without a fight.

"Oh dear me," Praiseworthy said. "You must tell me where I should set my course so I can perform the calculations and engage the rocket boosters!"

"We're going to Planet Royale!" Sarah shouted.

"No we're not!" Jacob yelled back. "Praiseworthy, if you head in that direction, I'm hitting the override. We're not going there."

"Jake . . ." Sarah said.

Jacob glared at her, and all of the feelings of the past couple of days came rushing back. "You got us into this mess by going along with that stupid pirate."

Sarah held up her hands. "I'm sorry, Jake, I—"

"How could you have done that to me? Do you have any idea how terrible Numonia was? It smelled like burp breath!"

Dexter nodded. "He's right about that. It really did smell like burp breath."

Jacob stared at Sarah with venom. "You ran off with that idiot pirate instead of taking care of your friends. Do you remember the pact? You're a liar."

"I'm sorry. I really am. You're right. I was wrong. But we came back for you, Jake! And we have to go to Planet Royale."

"Children!" Praiseworthy shouted. "Our enemies

are about to—" A huge cloud of dust shot out of the giant eraser. It surrounded the cockpit, and Praiseworthy began coughing. "It's . . . chalk dust . . . It's jamming my systems!"

"Stop this instant," a man said over the intercom. "This is the principal speaking. If you turn over Jacob *Voonderbar* you children may be on your way."

"Jake, hurry!" Sarah cried. "We have to go to Planet Royale!"

Jacob steeled his nerves and remembered his dad. "No. I'm not going back to Earth."

"Wonderbar . . ." Dexter said.

"I'm not going!"

"Why not?" Sarah cried.

Jacob took out the pipe. "Look at this. I found this in an antique shop on Planet Paisley. It's my dad's. It says 'Wonderbar' on it. My dad's out here somewhere in space, and I'm going to find him!"

Dexter and Sarah looked at each other like Jacob had lost his mind. "A pipe?" Sarah asked. "Jake, there's no time for this!"

"I saw Miss Banks!" Jacob said. "She was on Planet Paisley too. She was wearing jeans! If she's out there, maybe my dad is too."

"Miss Banks?" Dexter said. "Really?"

"Jake," Sarah said, "you can't go wandering around

the universe because you found a pipe. Or Miss Banks. That's crazy!"

"It's not crazy," Jacob said.

"Yes, it is!" Sarah glanced at the monitor, and the eraser was growing bigger and bigger.

Jacob gave her a cold stare. "You probably think I won't be able to find my dad. You probably think he just left me behind on purpose because I'm such a bad kid."

"I don't think that at all!" A little fire came back into her voice. "Look, I apologized to you, I meant it. You're not perfect either, you know. Who was the one who broke the universe? Not me!"

"Children," Praiseworthy said, "we have less than a minute before your enemies will be in range. We could be captured!"

The intercom buzzed. "We'd hate to use the ruler," an elderly woman said. "Just give us *Voonderbar* and we'll return to our crossword puzzles."

"Come on, Wonderbar!" Dexter pleaded.

"But I know he's out there," Jacob said, a little desperately. "And he's trying to find me. He's been trying to find me all this time. He just hasn't been able to get back home. I know it."

"Jake . . ." Sarah began.

"What?" he yelled.

Sarah took a deep breath, trying to calm herself. She wasn't going to fight. She would be calm and reasonable. Friends told each other the truth even when it was difficult to hear. She said as gently as she could, "Jake, your dad's not lost in space. He moved to Milwaukee. You know that's what happened."

"But how can you explain this?" He held up the pipe, less certain than before and starting to wonder if he was being ridiculous.

"A pipe?" Sarah asked.

Dexter put his hand on Jacob's shoulder, but he pulled away quickly. "Look. We all feel bad about your dad. We really do. And you might even be right about him looking for you."

"I *might* be right?" Jacob said a little hysterically.

The children held on to their seats as Praiseworthy began swooping and swerving in evasive maneuvers. "There's no time for this," Dexter said.

"Tell him, Dexter."

Jacob paused. "Tell me what?"

Dexter didn't say anything. He was still staring at the monitors.

"Tell me what?!"

He turned back to Jacob and took a deep breath. "I found out that my mom is in the hospital. It looked really bad. Cat's dad is the king of everything, and he can help us get home. Think about your mom and how scared she must be. We have to go home, Jacob. Right now."

Jacob pursed his lips together and rubbed his eyes.

There was suddenly movement on the eraser. A piece of the ship unfolded and a giant mechanical hand rose out of the top. It was clutching a massive ruler, and it looked as if it was ready to strike Praiseworthy.

"Children! They're going to be in range in moments! This has become a terribly urgent situation!"

Sarah stiffened her spine. They weren't going to be captured by a giant eraser or smashed by a large ruler on her watch.

"Praiseworthy, please set your course for Planet Royale," Sarah said firmly. "We need to talk to the king. He'll get us back to Earth."

"Master Wonderbar?" Praiseworthy asked.

Jacob stared at the floor. "Fine," he said.

Praiseworthy sighed with happiness and space blurred around the ship as he instantly fired his boosters. The eraser and its ruler faded into the distance.

Dexter exhaled in relief. "Oh, thank goodness."

It wasn't fair. Jacob had to travel billions of miles to have the smallest chance of finding his dad, and he felt even that slim possibility slipping away. He didn't understand why his dad couldn't come find him on

Earth, even just to visit once in a while to see how he was doing or take him to a baseball game. He wanted things to be like they used to be, with his father waiting for him when he came home from school and making sure he always had an exciting birthday. He never even called or e-mailed. Jacob's face crumpled, and he threw the pipe across the room. It smashed against the wall and fell to the floor.

"My dad's worthless."

Sarah and Dexter stared at the floor, not sure how to react.

Finally, Sarah tried to catch Jacob's eye. "I'm sorry, Jake. At least we're safe now."

Jacob didn't say anything.

Princess Catalina looked around at the three friends, her hands clasped tightly. "Um. Wow. Does anyone want some chocolate?"

CHAPTER 40

Jacob Wonderbar sank his teeth into the best beef jerky he had ever tasted in his life.

"Wow. Sven, you weren't kidding, this is really good."

Sven exhaled in relief. "Thank you, Mr. Wonderbar, thank you so much for saying that. I was really hoping you would like it, because our chef was worried that the smoker had not infused the perfect amount of flavor. He almost threw out the entire batch in a fit of despair and threatened to resign from his post before we convinced him to serve it. He was hysterical. I'll convey your compliments, and I know he will be extremely relieved."

Sven bowed and left. Jacob reclined in a wildly comfortable chaise longue on a balcony overlooking a beautiful lagoon surrounded by green trees. The pink marble walls of the palace rose up behind him, radiating the perfect amount of warmth. Jacob had to hand it to the king: He sure had a nice planet.

But Jacob wouldn't be staying long. He peeked around to see if anyone was watching, ran to the edge of the balcony, and then swung himself over the ledge. He began climbing down the ivy growing along the palace wall.

He had done his part. He had gotten Sarah and Dexter to Planet Royale and they could talk to the king and find their way home. But Jacob had no intention of going back to Earth. He would go and find Praiseworthy and hop on board and fly around space as long as he wanted, seeing new planets and stars and never going to school. Every now and then he'd visit Sarah and Dexter and his mom back on Earth, but space would be his new home. He would be an explorer or an adventurer or maybe even a better and more famous space pirate than Mick Cracken. Earth could wait.

He let go of the vine and dropped down to the ground. He slunk along the topiaries shaped like animals. He crouched behind a large boulder, ready to run.

"I thought you might try to escape," a familiar voice

said from the shadows. Mick Cracken stepped directly into Jacob's path. He was dressed in sharp black pants and a long black shirt. His hair was even combed.

"Ugh. You?" Jacob whispered. "What are you doing here?"

Mick's pained expression let in a hint of a grin. "Sarah didn't fill you in?"

"Fill me in on what? What are you trying to steal now?"

Mick waved his hand. "My dad owns the place."

"Owns this? But the king owns this."

"Uh-huh."

"But that means . . . That means you're the . . ." Jacob couldn't bring himself to say the word, and he felt his stomach twisting in knots. The idea of Mick wearing a crown and being addressed as "Your Eminence" or whatever they called princes in outer space was bad enough, but then it dawned on Jacob that if Mick was the prince, then someday he might be the king. Of the universe. "I think I'm going to be sick."

"Trust me, I don't like it any more than you do."

Jacob didn't have any time for Mick, even if he was the future king of everything. "Get out of the way. I'm leaving. I hope you trip over your crown or something."

Mick didn't move. "My dad wants to talk to you."

Jacob frowned. "Me?" He had no idea what he and the king could possibly talk about—or how the king even knew he existed.

"I think you should talk to him," Mick said.

Jacob looked carefully at Mick. The last time he had obeyed one of Mick's suggestions, he had ended up marooned on Numonia. "Is this another one of your traps?"

Mick's eyes glinted. "What the king wants, the king gets."

Jacob couldn't disagree with that logic.

CHAPTER 41

They reached the grand throne room, and Jacob saw where the king presided over everything. It was a huge gold chair in the center of the room, gilded with gems and lit from within, radiating bright light throughout the room. The throne was surrounded by brilliant old tapestries that depicted comets and stars throughout the universe. But the chair was empty.

"Where is he?" Jacob asked.

"Right here," a voice said.

Jacob turned around and looked up at a very tall man with a hearty white beard, with kind eyes and a wrinkled face. He was a bit on the portly side, and he wore a long white robe with a bright gold cloth stole.

"Hello, Jacob." He spoke with a faint accent. "My

name is King Alan Jones Dean Crackenarium. Would you please take a walk with me?"

He stepped out into the king's private gardens, which were impeccably trimmed and featured some of the most beautiful flowers he had ever seen. The hedges were perfectly green, and gray gravel crunched underneath his shoes. Brilliantly colored butterflies flew around and a large orange bird landed on Jacob's shoulder.

"Hi!" the bird said. "What's your name?"

Jacob gasped. "I . . . You can talk?!"

"Nice to meet you, Iyoucantalk! Bye!" The bird flew away.

Jacob turned to the king. "Why is space so weird?"

The king laughed a little. "I suppose space would seem strange to a child from Earth."

Jacob realized how little he knew about space. Nothing made sense. Space officers had refused to arrest them for destroying a huge amount of the universe. The Numonians loved their crazy planet where the days were a minute long. The scientists were excited about a joke involving a calculator. He had been to a planet full of terrifying substitute teachers. If space was going to be his new home, he needed to start understanding. "Where did all of this come from?" Jacob asked

The king smiled. "A long time ago there was a scientist who was tired of the war and the unhappiness and the strife on Planet Earth. He thought there could be something better out there, something different. So he built a spaceship. He blasted off with some of his friends, and left the old world behind. He was a great, wonderful man who loved life and made a better place for us. He left the problems behind on Earth and tried his best to create a utopia." The king waved his hand around. "We Astrals are his descendents, along with the people who have joined us in the years since then."

Jacob saw some red birds chasing one another around a tree, darting around and spinning in circles, laughing in high, chipper voices. "The man in silver said he found our town by accident and that the universe is fine. But that's not true, is it?" He turned back to the king, but he had knelt to sniff some flowers.

The king stood up and looked at Jacob as if he had just remembered he was there. "Someone wanted you to take this trip, Jacob Wonderbar. You noticed the coincidences. The spacesuits waiting for you aboard your ship, the tour of the solar system, the fact that you happened to run into your teacher. There are bigger things than you out there in the universe, and you are very, very special."

Jacob looked out at the puffy clouds in the distance. "My dad? Was it my dad?"

The king turned and kept walking. Jacob jogged a bit to catch up. "I'm concerned about the future. Astrals have developed strange ideas about Earth and they fear that Earth's problems will spread throughout the galaxies. Our societies have grown apart. Some think that Earth will bring war. I wanted to speak to a real Earther boy to see if I was still right about our mother planet's future. And who better than our substitute teachers' cleverest foe?"

Jacob's brow furrowed. "Do you mean . . ."

"Yes. I sent the man in silver. I wanted to meet you, Jacob."

The king stopped to examine a large bush cut in the shape of a giant bear. He plucked off a leaf and handed it to Jacob. It turned bright orange and dissolved in his hands. Jacob looked at the king to see if he was sending him a message, but the king still appeared lost in thought.

"There's a phrase in the Earth language French. It's called *joie de vivre*. Do you know what that means? It roughly translates to 'the joy of living.' Do you see how much the people in space love life? They pursue what they love, they always have a great time. They have moved past so many of the problems of Earth. But sometimes they get so caught up in having fun and chasing after the things that interest them, they forget that there is a time for *joie de vivre* and there is a time for responsibility. Astrals are not perfect either."

Jacob nodded. "That's why I'm staying here in space. Jaw-de-veeve."

"You don't want to go back to Earth?"

Jacob shook his head.

But then he had a sudden image of his mom out of her mind with panic about him disappearing, and he couldn't bear to think of her living alone in the house. Even if being gone would have meant less stress and fewer visits to Mr. Bradley's office, he knew she would be lonely. And he would need to be there if Dexter had to visit his mom in the hospital, especially since hospitals contained a wide variety of items that could cause Dexter to pass out, including needles, blood, the smell of latex, tongue depressors, and hairnets. He held out a bit of hope that if he went home now, at least he could find a way to get back into space at some point and have more adventures.

"Maybe I can just visit Earth sometimes?"

"I can send you back to Earth," the king said with a faint smile. "But it won't be on a spaceship. It would be a one-way trip."

Jacob's heart sank. Every atom in his body wanted

to stay in outer space, to go out and have more adventures and find new planets, and possibly find someone who had disappeared from his life. He looked at the ground. "Is my dad in space?"

The king rubbed his beard. "It's not for me to say, Jacob."

Even with the possibility, however faint, that his dad might be out there somewhere in space, Jacob was beginning to accept what he had to do. He had to go back with his friends so they could be there for one another back on Earth. He had to give up on what he wanted so that he could do the right thing for them and for his mom, who put up with him all those times he was sent home from school. He suddenly realized that he never even apologized for making her miss her meeting.

"We should go home," he said quietly.

The king grasped Jacob by the shoulders. "That's why you're the hero, Jacob Wonderbar. The universe has big plans for you."

Jacob looked around at birds and butterflies, the huge stone fountains, the marble palace, the palm trees, and the turquoise lagoon. "Will I get to come back to space?"

The king's eyes crinkled. "If I need you, I will find you."

The king stepped back and Jacob saw Sarah standing in the garden, looking a bit bashful as she waited for him. He watched the king as he walked away, and Sarah bounded over.

"What did he say?" she asked.

"He said that I'm the . . ." Jacob trailed off. "He said we're going home. All of us."

Sarah whooped and hugged Jacob tightly. He never seemed to remember how strong she was until she did something violent. "I'm so happy, I'm so happy, I'm so happy, I'm so happy," she said into his chest.

Jacob tried to talk through her tight embrace. "I'm sorry I was so mean on the spaceship," he said. "And thank you for rescuing me from the subs. It's just been . . ."

"I'm sorry too," she said, pulling back and looking him in the eyes. "Really. For chasing after the stupid diamond and not coming back for you right away. I'm always off doing other things. You're the most important person in the world to me, and . . ." Sarah held her hands to her lips like she had said too much.

Jacob couldn't think of anything to say. He was so happy, he felt like he had taken leave of his body. She saw the look on his face and punched him hard on the shoulder.

"You're supposed to say something nice back, loser."

265

"Sorry."

"We'll work on that."

Sarah's expression grew serious and she stopped and held up a finger. She took something out of her pocket and pressed it into Jacob's hand. It was the pipe. He felt the familiar smooth wood and the slightly rough pewter. He turned it over and looked at the inscription.

He felt so lucky to have Sarah, the type of friend who knew when something like a pipe needed to be saved rather than lost again out in the universe.

"Your dad misses you, Jake. I know he does."

Jacob stared at it for a while. He finally said, "Thanks, Sarah."

She smiled back and laughed. "Now let's go home."

CHAPTER 42

Dexter stared at the machine that was going to send them back to Earth. It looked like a scary elevator or a bank safe, with three metal sides and a thick door, but to Dexter it looked more like a medieval torture device. "Um. How does this work exactly?"

The attending scientist said, "We're going to beam all of the atoms in your body through a wormhole and include a code that will reassemble them in the exact order back on Earth."

Dexter tried not to hyperventilate. "No way. Nuh-uh. That's what they did in *Charlie in the Chocolate Factory* and Mike Teavee got shrunk!"

Sarah sighed. "They're not going to shrink us, Dexter."

"How do you know?"

The royal family had gathered around as Dexter,

Sarah, and Jacob prepared to leave. Princess Catalina walked over and gave Jacob a long hug and three air kisses on his cheek. "Good-bye, my future husband. Stay handsome."

Sarah gritted her teeth and hoped that Jacob Wonderbar wasn't getting any ideas. Princess Catalina broke the hug and walked slowly away, flipping her hair at Sarah. "If you get tired of Earth girls, come back and find me."

Sarah thought about tearing the princess limb from limb, but she contented herself by remembering that she was going back to Earth with Jacob, and Catalina wasn't.

Catalina gave Dexter a long hug and said, "Your mom will be fine, okay?"

She walked over to Sarah, who stiffened as Princess Catalina air-kissed her. "Good-bye, darling. Let's work on that fashion, mmkay?"

"You work on your personality," Sarah muttered. Princess Catalina laughed like she had just heard the best joke in the universe.

The king stepped over to Jacob and leaned down to speak to him. "Remember what I said, young Jacob. I see wonderful things in your future."

Jacob looked over at Mick and thought he saw him stand a little taller, a sliver of disappointment cross-

ing his face. But Jacob's chest filled with pride that the king of everything had such confidence in him. "Thank you, Your Majesty."

The children waited for Mick to come and say his good-byes, but instead he just stood there impassively, refusing to move.

Sarah cleared her throat, but he just stared straight ahead with a sour expression. Sarah grew tired of waiting and she walked over and gave him a hug.

"Thanks for the adventures, Cracken."

Mick smiled bashfully and said, "We'll get that diamond."

Jacob decided to set aside his grievances and walked over to offer Mick a handshake. "For the record, I completely knew you were lying about the Dragon's Eye."

"You're a worthy opponent," Mick said, shaking his hand.

"If you happen to steal a spaceship, I wouldn't mind showing you around Earth," Jacob said.

"Michaelus is done stealing spaceships for a while," the king said.

Mick glared at his dad for a moment and then went back to staring at his shoes.

Jacob looked around at his friends. They nodded in agreement and stepped into the chamber. They were finally going home.

Sarah held Dexter's hand to give him extra bravery. They waved good-bye to the royal family. The scientist slowly closed the door.

"You won't feel a . . ."

The children were standing at the edge of the forest on their block on the street where all the houses looked the same. The air was still slightly warm, and the orange moon was shining brightly. Fireflies were flickering all around.

Jacob reacted first, falling to the ground and pressing his face to the street.

"Asphalt . . ." he sighed. "Earth asphaaaalt."

"We're back home!" Sarah yelled.

Jacob stood up and joined them as they jumped up and down and hugged. They stopped and looked at one another, so happy and relieved that they had finally made it. Now that they were back, they noticed that Earth actually had a unique smell. Kind of like dirt, but a little sweet.

"New pact," Jacob said, putting out his hand. "Space friends forever."

Sarah and Dexter put their hands over Jacob's. "Space friends forever!"

Dexter stepped away and his smile faded as he thought about his mom. "I gotta go, guys."

Sarah grabbed his hand. "We're going together."

They ran toward Dexter's house, and though he was worried about Dexter's mom, Jacob couldn't help but wonder how much trouble they would be in. There weren't police officers around Dexter's house, and he realized they must have gone home for the day. News crews would probably show up soon and want to interview them about their mysterious disappearance.

They reached the door to Dexter's house and nearly

collided into it when it swung open. Dexter's mom peered down at them, her hair in its customary bun. She looked perfectly healthy.

"Mom!" Dexter shouted. "You're not in the hospital!"

"The hospital? Why would I be in the hospital?" Dexter's mom frowned at Jacob. "Jacob Wonderbar, is this another one of your pranks?"

"But . . ." Dexter said. "Aren't you . . ."

"No 'buts,'" Dexter's mom said. "It's time for you children to get on home." She pulled Dexter inside and closed the door.

Sarah's eyes were wide. "What just happened?"

"I . . . I don't know."

"I should go home," she said. She gave Jacob one last hug and said, "See you, Jake." She ran toward her house.

Jacob walked home slowly. He imagined the hysteria that would await him when he arrived. His mom would probably cry, and he hated seeing his mom cry. He wondered if there was a way of entering that wouldn't result in screams and burst eardrums. He stared at his door and summoned his strength. He could do this. He knew his mom would simply be overjoyed to see him. He opened it and walked in.

"Mom, I'm so sorry, I—"

"That was fast." He saw his mom sitting at the kitchen table, sipping some apple juice.

"Fast?! Are you . . ."

"No more corndogs, kiddo. If you want more food, there's leftover tuna surprise in the fridge."

"I . . ."

"You can watch a half hour of TV, but then it's bedtime, okay?"

"I . . ."

"No arguing, Jacob! Half hour and then it's bedtime. I have to go upstairs and check on the Asian markets again, and when I come back, I want you in your pajamas and ready for bed."

No time had passed, he quickly realized. His mom wasn't surprised in the least to see him.

It wasn't possible. There had to have been a mistake. He wondered if he had imagined the whole thing.

He reached into his pocket.

He felt his dad's pipe.

"Hey Mom!" Jacob shouted.

"Hmm?" she asked from the top of the stairs.

Jacob thought about telling her everything, about finding the pipe and meeting the king and what the stars looked like when he spacewalked. "I'm sorry I made you miss your meeting."

His mom smiled. "Thanks, Jacob. That was a very mature thing to say." She kept walking. "You're still grounded though."

CHAPTER 43

"Good morning, class," Mrs. Pinkerton warbled.

"Good morning, Mrs. Pinkerton," the class repeated.

"Class, there has been a slight . . . change of plans. Your teacher Miss Banks has . . . well . . . she won't be here for a while. I'll be your teacher until further notice, so *get used to it!*" She rapped the table with her ruler, and every spine in the class snapped to attention.

Jacob, Sarah, and Dexter looked around at one another, smiling but a little bewildered. Jacob hoped that Miss Banks would be okay on Planet Paisley.

Mrs. Pinkerton cleared her throat, giving Jacob goose bumps.

"Today we're going to discuss the solar system. Jacob Wonderbar, could you please tell the class which is the smallest planet in the solar system?"

"Numonia," Jacob said confidently.

Dexter buried his face in his hands and tried not to laugh. Sarah cackled.

"I hear they have nice space dust though," Jacob added. His classmates laughed nervously, ready for one of Jacob's pranks.

Mrs. Pinkerton glided over to Jacob's desk, and he caught a whiff of her breath, which happened to have been heavier on burned coffee than rotten eggs that morning. "Do you think this is a joke?" She tapped her ruler against her palm as if she were considering using it as a weapon.

"No ma'am," Jacob said, trying to keep a straight face.

"Because we both know that Numonia is not *in* the solar system."

"So you've heard of Numonia?"

Mrs. Pinkerton's eyes narrowed and she cleared her voice. "Why, uh, no. As a matter of fact, I have . . . Numonia you say?" She leaned forward and said, "Well played, Mr. Wonderbar. Or should I say, *Voonderbar*?" His classmates laughed when she said it, but a shiver went down Jacob's neck.

Mrs. Pinkerton slowly walked back to the front of

the class and glared at Jacob. "You'd better watch your step."

She then launched into a detailed lecture on the planets of the solar system. Jacob noticed in particular how she seemed to relish talking about how unremarkable the sun and Earth were compared to the vast variety of other stars and planets throughout the universe.

The bell rang an agonizing hour later, and at recess, Jacob, Dexter, and Sarah huddled together. Kids were bustling around, chatting and playing soccer, but Jacob felt like he hardly knew them anymore. They didn't even realize there were spaceships that flew far into outer space and planets full of wacky space humans. But he wasn't about to tell his classmates. They'd just think he was insane.

"Dexter, your mom really isn't sick?" Jacob asked.

"She's fine! I can't believe it. It was the same as before I left. I think the king cured her or something."

Sarah cocked her head. "Can the king do that?

"I don't know, I just assumed because he's the king and all . . . Anyway, when I got home she gave me and my dad a huge lecture about how used paper towels always go in the compost bin, so really I think she's fine."

"Wow, that's great," Jacob said.

"That *is* great," Sarah said. "I was hoping I had

missed my piano recital because I haven't had time to practice, but . . . well, that is most definitely on." A soccer ball from a nearby game rolled over toward them, and Sarah sent it back with a perfect, effortless kick.

"I'm still grounded too," Jacob said. "I was kind of hoping my mom would be so overjoyed to see me that she would have forgotten about all of that, but she didn't even notice I was gone."

Sarah grunted in agreement. "After I realized it was still a couple of days ago or whatever, I talked to my parents about cutting back on just a few of my extra-curriculars to spend some more time with you guys." She darted her eyes at Jacob. "I mean, because of my stress levels. I didn't even ask to quit everything, because I know I'd be bored if I did. I just want to cut back a little."

"What did they say?" Jacob asked quickly. The idea of having more time with Sarah was terrifically exciting, and his heart was very anxious to know how fast it should beat depending on the news.

"不可能"

"What does that mean?"

Sarah sighed. "It means 'no way' in Mandarin."

CHAPTER 44

Later that night, after finishing her homework and piano practice, Sarah slipped out her front door and walked down the street. She knocked on Dexter's door, Dexter successfully negotiated with his mother for a half hour of free time, and they walked together over to Jacob Wonderbar's house. Jacob smiled when he saw them and snuck outside when his mom wasn't watching. A couple of minutes later they were lying on their backs on Jacob's front lawn, staring up at the sky. Jacob and Sarah lay next to each other, their shoulders just touching, and Dexter was a few feet away.

Jacob looked up at the stars, twinkling and almost friendly, and it felt so incredible to think that he had flown among them just yesterday. Other than some light pollution from the city, it was basically the same canopy of dotted light they had seen out of spaceship windows or when it was night on Numonia.

Jacob squinted up to see if he could spot the Spilled Milky Way galaxy. It had seemed so impossibly huge when they were close to it, but the most he could see in the sky was a faint smudge that could have been anything.

Dexter giggled. "What do you think Mick Cracken is doing right now?"

Sarah smiled. "He's probably trying to figure out how to lock Princess Pointyhead in a basement somewhere."

"I bet he's trying to find a diamond bigger than the Dragon's Eye so that he can steal that," Jacob said.

"No way," Dexter said. "I bet he's all depressed in his palace because he misses us so much.'"

Then things were quiet again except for the sound of crickets and frogs. Jacob ran his hands through the tips of the grass, which tickled a little and had the faintest bit of dew.

"If you could go back into space," Sarah said, "would you do it?"

"I would," Jacob said as casually as he could. "What about you?"

Sarah laughed. "I might buy a box of corndogs just in case the man in silver comes back."

They both looked over at Dexter, lost in thought and staring up at the stars.

He smiled. "Definitely."

Jacob looked at Sarah out of the corner of his eye, and then scrunched his body just a couple of millimeters closer. She did the same.

He closed his eyes and remembered what it felt like to whoosh around in space, breathing the faintly metallic air inside the spaceships and feeling the floor shudder as Praiseworthy went as fast as he could go. He could almost hear the quiet hum of the engines and feel the slight tug when they whipped around in a turn and could still remember the way passing planets looked like colorful crescents.

He didn't know if he would ever have the chance to fly through space again, but the twinkling stars would always make him remember that he had been there with his best friends.

And whether his dad was in outer space or Milwaukee, Jacob knew that his view was probably the same.

ACKNOWLEDGMENTS

JACOB WONDERBAR would have never made it off the ground if it weren't for my incredible crew:

NAVIGATION: Innumerable thanks to my fantastic agent, Catherine Drayton, and my amazing editor, Kate Harrison, for always keeping me on the right course.

LOGISTICS: Thanks to Heather Alexander, Patricia Burke, Lyndsey Blessing, Alexis Hurley, Nathaniel Jacks, and Charlie Olson for making sure things were always running smoothly.

DESIGN: Thanks to Jasmin Rubero (interior), Greg Stadnyk (cover), and Christopher S. Jennings (illustrations) for making Wonderbar come to life.

FUEL: Special thanks to Philz Coffee of San Francisco, whose delicious Jacob's Wonderbar Brew kept me going on many a Saturday morning.

GROUND SUPPORT: I couldn't ask for two more incredible families, the Bransfords and the Presleys, and am constantly thankful for their love and support. Thanks also to Justin Berkman, Egya Appiah, Sean Slinsky and Holly Burns, Bryan Russell, Peter Ginsberg, Laura Blake Peterson, and all my friends at Curtis Brown Ltd.

CO-PILOT: Alison Presley. I'll go anywhere in the universe as long as you're by my side.